WHISTLER'S MOTHER'S SON

and Other Curiosities

Peter Cherches

PELEKINESIS

NEW YORK † LONDON † SYDNEY † LOS ANGELES

Praise for *Whistler's Mother's Son*

"I love to read Peter Cherches' world always, but sometimes I feel like I'm a character in it. Help me! I'm stuck inside a Peter Cherches blurb! Liltingly bizarre, awesomely askew, and funnyfunnyfunny!"

– Bob Holman

"Minimalist wit has never been so maximal in effect or ambit. Cherches' ironies don't obey the sidewalk law of step on a crack and you'll break your mother's back. They put their feet down solid and exact—chunky, radiant, double-comprendres and paradoxes made terse. Apart from Peter Cherches, I don't know where you'll find nuggets of gold and fool's gold as crazy-true-and-false as these."

– Rafi Zabor, author of *The Bear Comes Home*

Praise for Peter Cherches' previous books

Lift Your Right Arm:

"One of the innovators of the short short story, Cherches (*Condensed Book*) returns with a collection whose pieces linger in the void somewhere between poetry and prose. Consisting of five sequences of loosely connected minimalist stories—few of which go on for longer than a page—these "novellas," though distinct, keep returning to certain overarching themes: the reality of death, the difficulty of expressing subjective perspective, and the failures of language."

– *Publishers Weekly*

"Packed into *Lift Your Right Arm* are conundrums, Abbott-and-Costello dialogues, nonsense narratives and other playful—sometimes hilarious, sometimes subversive—assaults on logic. To Gödel, Escher, and Bach we might consider adding Peter Cherches."

– Billy Collins

"Peter Cherches is one of the stingiest writers going—stingy with words, that is. He won't use ten words if he can get away with five, and he won't write a novel if he can convey its pith in a page. This book, then, is the equivalent of a whole shelf of books. Read slowly, it can last you for years."

– Luc Sante

Autobiography Without Words:

"In *Autobiography Without Words*, a tongue-in-cheek, fragmented, fictionalized memoir, author Peter Cherches taps memory with wit and whimsy to whip up a fractured mosaic of self."

– Peter Wortsman, author of *A Modern Way to Die*

"Peter Cherches's collection of flashes, *Autobiography Without Words*, has a lot of words in it. It is also not a typical autobiography—more a hallucinatory romp through Jewishness, New York City, and the surreal side of satire.... [I]f you like funny, if you like wry, if you like a healthy dollop of rather un-nostalgic nostalgia, this book is perfect."

– Jonathan Cardew, *Flash Magazine*

Whistler's Mother's Son and Other Curiosities by Peter Cherches

ISBN: 978-1-949790-17-7
eISBN: 978-1-949790-18-4

"In the Bush" (Adams/ Cooper) © 1978 Universal Music Publishing Group

"(I'll Be With You) In Apple Blossom Time" (Von Tilzer/ Fleeson) © 1920 Jerry Vogel Music Co. Inc, Sony/ATV Music Publishing LLC

Layout and book design by Mark Givens
Cover design and artwork by Allan Bealy
Author photo by Elder Zamora

First Pelekinesis Printing 2020

For information: **Pelekinesis**
112 Harvard Ave #65, Claremont, CA 91711 USA

Library of Congress Cataloging-in-Publication Data

Names: Cherches, Peter, author.
Title: Whistler's mother's son : and other curiosities / Peter Cherches.
Other titles: Prose works. Selections
Description: Claremont : Pelekinesis, 2020.
Identifiers: LCCN 2019035570 (print) | LCCN 2019035571 (ebook) | ISBN 9781949790177 (paperback) | ISBN 9781949790184 (epub)
Classification: LCC PS3553.H3527 A6 2020 (print) | LCC PS3553.H3527 (ebook) | DDC 818/.5407--dc23
LC record available at https://lccn.loc.gov/2019035570
LC ebook record available at https://lccn.loc.gov/2019035571

www.pelekinesis.com

Whistler's Mother's Son
and Other Curiosities

_____

Peter Cherches

Grateful acknowledgment is made to the following journals, anthologies and websites in which many of these pieces originally appeared, often in slightly or greatly different form, and occasionally under different titles:

3:AM, Another Chicago Magazine, Asylum Annual, Barney, Benzene, Between C & D, The Big Book of New American Humor, Black Scat Review, Blatant Artifice, Book Post, The Cafe Irreal, Central Park, Danse Macabre, Diana's Third Almanac, Eclectica, Five Plus Five, Flash, Flash Fiction Funny, Flash Fire 500, Funny Bone, Games, Hambone, Harper's, High Times, Insurance, The Journal of Compressed Creative Arts, Kiosk, The Low Tech Manual, MungBeing, New Observations, North American Review, Oddity, Offbeat & Quirky, Qarrtsiluni, Red Tape, Revolution John, Rumble, Semiotext(e), Shiny International, Six Little Things, Six Sentences, Snow Monkey, Tenth Assembling, Tuesday Shorts, Unbearables, Unlost.

"Unfamiliar Tales" was originally published in a limited edition by Purgatory Pie Press.

Performance versions of "Kennedy's Brain" and "It's Uncle!" can be heard on the digital release *It's Uncle!* by Peter Cherches & Sonorexia.

A special thanks to all the writers who provided original texts for the collaborations section.

Contents

In memory of Holly Anderson, friend, collaborator, inspiration.

Whistler's Mother's Son

The painting known as "Whistler's Mother" gave birth to a son, a painting of the painter James Abbott McNeill Whistler. The painting of Whistler, in turn, painted a painting of its mother, the painting of Whistler's mother. This painting, the painting of the painting of Whistler's mother, painted by the painting of Whistler the painter, gave birth, but this time to a daughter, a flesh and blood daughter who turned out to be the real-life Whistler's mother. This daughter, Whistler's mother, gave birth to a son named James Abbott McNeill Whistler, who immortalized her in a painting known as "Arrangement in Gray and Black Number 1."

The Invention of Catch

After Miro

    A man threw a stone at a bird, and the bird threw it back, and the man threw it back at the bird, and the bird threw it back at the man, and the man once again threw the stone at the bird, and the bird once again threw the stone at the man, and the man threw it back, and the bird threw it back, and the man and the bird threw the stone back and forth.

In the Cave of Signed Paintings

In the cave of signed paintings, all the paintings are signed with paintings of cave paintings.

The Flintstone Variations

"It's language that sets us apart from the beasts," says Fred Flintstone.

"Nothing sets you apart from the beasts," Wilma replies.

*   *   *

On the radio, three critics are discussing cave paintings. One contends that they're primitive, another that they're neo-primitive, and the third that they're not primitive at all, that they're as modern as the wheel. All this intellectual talk bores Fred Flintstone. Besides, he prefers Norman Rockwell.

*   *   *

Later that night, Fred and Wilma fuck. Fred prefers the bronto position. In fact, most prehistoric men prefer the bronto position.

*   *   *

Fred and Wilma go to the movies. It is a foreign film, one by Stoneyoni. None of the cave men in the audience understand it, and when the film is over they all demand their money back. A scuffle ensues in which several die. That's why the Flintstones like to go to foreign films—you can always count on a scuffle.

*   *   *

The Flintstones take a vacation. They go to visit the Grand Canyon. When they arrive they're disappointed. The "canyon" is nothing more than a shallow trench, hardly what you'd call "grand." They send a picture postcard to the Rubbles. The Rubbles agree that the Grand Canyon is nothing to write home about, but they're fascinated by the concept of picture postcards.

*   *   *

Though undeniably a "modern stone-age kind of guy," Fred Flintstone still retains vestiges of an earlier code. While he does speak English, a sure sign of civilization, he often interjects into his speech a particular preliterate utterance— "yabba dabba doo." What precisely is the meaning of "yabba dabba doo"? This question has occupied the attentions of paleontologists and linguists alike for many years. What is perhaps the most plausible theory is that "yabba dabba doo" is a mating call, a holdover from a time when Man could not express his excitement in a more socially acceptable manner, such as, "Ooh baby, you really turn me on."

*   *   *

The town of Bedrock is up in arms. A family of Barbarians is trying to move into this neat suburban community. An incensed Fred and Barney decide to take matters into their own hands. They storm the house that the Barbarians are planning to move into. Coincidentally, the Barbarians are inside, taking measurements. What a stroke of luck. Fred and Barney attack the Barbarians, rip their bodies to pieces with their bare hands, and eat of their flesh.

*   *   *

THE DISCOVERY OF FIRE

Fred Flintstone feels fresh fruit furtively. Fred Flintstone frames famous Flemish frescoes. Fred Flintstone flaunts frilly feminine fashions. Fred Flintstone frenches flaming Franciscan friars. Fred Flintstone fondles Frieda Fleischman, floozie. Fred Flintstone fears fever from festering foreskin. Fred Flintstone finds Fassbinder's films fascinating. Fred Flintstone finds Fielding's fiction funny. Fred Flintstone finds Flaubert's fiction fluid. Fred Flintstone finds Fitzgerald's fiction fabulous. Fred Flintstone finds Faulkner's fiction frightening. Fred Flintstone finds fire.

*   *   *

The doorbell rings and Fred runs to answer it. It's a couple of Jehovah's Witnesses. "We're not interested," Fred says, and tries to close the door on them.

"Wait!" one of the Witnesses says. "We know when the world is going to end."

"Gimme a break," Fred says. "It only just started a little while ago."

*　　*　　*

Something is bothering Fred Flintstone. He can't put his finger on it, but something is definitely bothering him. Wilma notices. "Is something wrong?" she asks.

"Yes," Fred replies, "something is wrong, but I don't know what it is." And then, all of a sudden, he begins to cry, uncontrollably. Wilma tries to comfort him, and in time Fred stops crying. Embarrassed, Fred apologizes for losing control.

"That's okay, dear," Wilma says. "These days it's all right for a cave man to cry."

Passed Out

As I left my building for a walk one Saturday morning, I saw a bunch of people standing around in a circle, looking down at the pavement. I figured whatever it was, there were enough people to take care of it, no need for another gawker, but still I was curious.

"What happened?" I asked a woman as I went to join the circle.

"I don't know, he was just lying there."

I wondered who it was. Perhaps one of my neighbors? It was, after all, right in front of my building. I couldn't get a good look at the guy until I moved further into the circle. Then I saw who it was. It was me!

What was the meaning of this? How was I lying unconscious in front of my building and looking at myself from above at the same time? I was wearing the same clothes, the unconscious me and the conscious me. The standing, conscious me had no memory of anything happening to myself that could have caused me to be lying on the pavement.

"Does anybody know his name?" someone called out.

"Yes," I said, "it's me! Peter Cherches!"

"Peter Cherches? That's a funny name for a dog," someone else said.

Dog? I thought. Then I took another look. It was a big, mangy, stray dog passed out on the pavement, not me at all.

Embarrassed, I slunk away from the circle and then ran as fast and as far as my four legs would take me.

A One-Woman Show

She exhibited a ghastly pallor in the gallery. It was her first one-woman show, and she was nervous, fortunately, because her nervousness was the entire show, a conceptual installation, "A Nervous Artist." It was the genuineness, the honesty of her nervousness that made the show the great success that it was. All the reviews were favorable: They spoke of the work's essential humanity; they spoke of how the artist and her art were inseparable, yet this was not entirely the case, because the artist's nervousness was such a hit that she sold it to a collector for a great deal of money. She was very calm at the opening of her second show, "The Artist at Ease," and this show was an even greater success than her first, her calm selling for three times as much as her nervousness. Her third show was a retrospective.

Dissatisfaction

A man who was dissatisfied with his penis went to the movies one sunny day. As it was a sunny day, the movie theater was empty. As the movie theater was empty, the projectionist did not notice that the man who was dissatisfied with his penis was in the audience, so he didn't run the film. The man who was dissatisfied with his penis was very upset. Not only do I have an unsatisfactory penis, he thought, but I am sitting in a dark, silent movie theater, missing a perfectly beautiful day. At which point he decided to ask for his money back. He went to the ticket booth and said to the girl, "I would like my money back, as they are not showing the film, and I would like to enjoy this nice, sunny day."

"Very well," the girl said, "just show me your penis and I'll be happy to refund your money."

At which point the man ran off, crying, cursing his penis, twelve dollars poorer and unable to enjoy a beautiful day.

The Man with a Steak Nose

There once was a man whose nose was made of steak. It was a T-bone steak, this man's nose—a big, red, raw T-bone steak. In all other respects he was completely normal.

When he walked down the street people always stared at him because of his steak nose. People stared because it was not usual to see a man with a steak for a nose. Most of them meant no harm, they just couldn't help staring. Some people—steak lovers—stared at him longingly, because his nose reminded them of how much they loved steak. Others—vegetarians—stared at him angrily, because the man's nose reminded them of meat eaters. He tried not to let it bother him.

The steak-nose man led a fairly normal life. He had a job in an office, and he got along well with most of his office mates. Most of them got so used to the steak nose that they forgot there was anything unusual about the man.

Sometimes the man was a little sad because his nose was made of steak, but most of the time he didn't even think about it.

One day the man decided he would like a pet dog, to keep him company. When he walked into the pet shop, all the dogs started barking when they smelled his steak nose. He chose a cute little dachshund. He brought it home and named it Frank.

The man and Frank quickly formed a strong bond. You could say they loved each other.

The steak-nose man's friends at the office were very happy for him now that he had Frank, because they knew that he had been lonely, even if he never said it.

One day, several weeks after the man had bought Frank, they were play-wrestling. The man nuzzled his face with Frank's, and Frank bit off a big chunk of his steak nose.

Frank chewed on the piece of steak and the man saw that Frank was very happy.

The man was both sad and happy: sad because he was now missing a big chunk of his nose, happy because Frank was happy.

Kennedy's Brain

I take the jar down from the shelf and stare at Kennedy's brain. Kennedy's brain. In a jar. In formaldehyde. I bought it for $3.95. I know it's not really Kennedy's brain. I'm not stupid. I know you can't get Kennedy's brain for $3.95. It is a real brain, though. A reasonable facsimile of Kennedy's brain.

Why do I stare at Kennedy's brain? I loaned my guitar to Eddie, so now I stare at Kennedy's brain.

My next-door neighbors are Indians. From India. From Calcutta. They fight a lot. They make a lot of noise. I always hear them fighting when I'm staring at Kennedy's brain. I get off on the sound. I can't hear the words, but the sound is something else.

> My neighbors are from Calcutta,
> Their apartment is full of clutta,
> They fight all the time,
> When I'm staring at Kennedy's brain.

Television. It's the light. That bluish-gray light of television. Black and white. Best kind of light to watch Kennedy's brain by. No sound. I've got all the sound I need. My neighbors take care of that. I just need the light. It doesn't matter what's on. It's just got to be on.

Kennedy's brain. I stare at it for hours. By the light of the television. To the sound of my neighbors. In the absence of anything else to do. And when I'm through, I put the jar back on the shelf.

> Kennedy's brain.
> Kennedy's brain.
> Kennedy's brain.

It's Uncle!

It's Uncle! Uncle has arrived! Uncle is here!
It's Uncle! Uncle has arrived! Uncle is here!
Hello Uncle! Hello Uncle! Hello Uncle!
Boy, are we glad to see you.
And I'm glad to see all of you.
Are you really, Uncle? Are you really glad to see all of us?
Of course I'm glad to see all of you. I'm always glad to see all of you.
And we're always glad to see you, Uncle.
I know. I'm always glad to see all of you, and all of you are always glad to see me, and we're all always glad to see each other. All of us.
It's Uncle! Uncle has arrived! Uncle is here!
It's Uncle! Uncle has arrived! Uncle is here!
All of us. Each and every one of us is glad to see each other. We're all glad to see each other.
Not me! I ain't glad to see ya, says Father. I ain't in the least bit glad to see ya. I wouldn't care if I never saw you again. You could rot in Hell, for all I care. I ain't glad to see ya. Not me. I ain't in the least bit glad to see ya.
Why can't you be nice once in a while? Says Mother. To Father. Why do you always have to be so nasty? You're always so nasty. Why can't you be nice once in a while? Says Mother. To Father.
It's his nature to be nasty. Says Uncle, to Mother, of Father.
Who ya callin' nasty? says Father. He's angry. He's mad. He's incensed.
He's fuming, boiling, raging, fierce. Wild, furious, fiery, rabid. Flushed with anger. Foaming at the mouth. He's turning red. Gritting his teeth. Clenching his fists. He's ready to explode!

You wanna fight?

You wanna fight?

You wanna fight you wanna fight you wanna fight?

And Uncle says, I didn't come here to fight.

Then why did you come here? says Father.

It's Uncle! Uncle has arrived! Uncle is here!

It's Uncle! Uncle has arrived! Uncle is here!

Hello Uncle! Hello Uncle! Hello Uncle!

Uncle has arrived and we're all glad to see him. All of us, that is, except for Father, who is not glad to see him.

It's Uncle! It's Uncle! It's Uncle!

Are you glad to see me? says Uncle.

Of course, Uncle, of course. Of course, Uncle, of course. Of course, Uncle, of course. We're all glad to see you.

Some of us, that is.

Reading Comprehension

I.

Twentieth-century Americans are happier than our ancestors because we have more to be happy about. Also, there are more of us to be happy, so the country is happier as a whole. We have many things to be happy about, but the happiest thing of all is that we are Americans.

Today's American is happier than yesterday's American because life is easier. Our forefathers, those great men who built our nation, did not always have it so easy. Building a nation is hard work, and it doesn't pay very well, so many of our forefathers had to go hungry. Today, no American need be hungry. All Americans eat well because of the sacrifices made by the architects of our great nation. Our great nation was built by many hungry men. George Washington was just one of them.

Life today is also easier than in the past because of the many wonderful inventions that make life easier for all of us. These inventions are the result of American ingenuity. All great inventions are American. Those great American inventors, such as Edison, Bell, and Marconi, were able to make their important discoveries because of the sacrifices of our forefathers. We can watch television and use our electric can openers because Thomas Jefferson often went to bed without supper.

America is the land of opportunity. In America, anybody can become an inventor. For instance, the peanut was invented by a Negro.

Things are very different in Russia. The people in Russia are not happy. In fact, the people in Russia used to be much happier. This is because they used to be ruled by a happy ruler known as the Czar. Now they are ruled by a group of unhappy rulers known as the Communists.

Many Russians go to bed without supper. This is very sad, but very true.

1. A good title for this passage would be:

    a) Thomas Edison, Inventor
    b) Thomas Jefferson, Martyr
    c) The Negro Problem
    d) Hunger and Happiness

2. The main idea of this passage is:

    a) America is good
    b) Inventions are good
    c) Russia is bad
    d) All of the above

3. Thomas Jefferson went to bed without supper because:

    a) He went to bed with his slaves
    b) He was on a diet
    c) He wanted us to be happy
    d) Alexander Graham Bell invented the telephone
    e) a & c

4. We can watch television because:

    a) America is a free country
    b) The Russians haven't figured out how to jam the airwaves
    c) It was invented by an American
    d) None of the above

5. The rulers of Russia are unhappy because:

    a) They're Communists
    b) They're not American
    c) They know they can't win the Cold War
    d) All of the above

II.

Juanita and her family have recently come to America. America is better than where Juanita comes from. Juanita does not know this, but she will learn, just as she will learn to speak English poorly. Juanita does not understand why she had to leave her old home, but someday she will learn. The first thing she must learn is not to ask questions.

Juanita lives in Cleveland. Cleveland is a city in Iowa. There are many little girls in Cleveland, Iowa, just as there are many little boys where Juanita comes from. Juanita comes from somewhere else. It is better here than where Juanita comes from.

Juanita goes to school in Cleveland. She is in first grade. She is older than most of her classmates, but this is because she is from somewhere else. Most of Juanita's classmates were born in Cleveland, Iowa. Juanita's classmates laugh at her because she pronounces Iowa incorrectly. Juanita says "Ohio." Juanita's classmates laugh when she says Ohio. Children can be cruel.

Juanita thinks that where she comes from is better than America because where she comes from the little girls don't laugh at her. She also likes where she comes from better because where she comes from there are many little boys. There are no little boys in Cleveland, Iowa. Someday Juanita will learn there is no justice in this world.

America is better than where Juanita comes from. Cleveland, Iowa, is a very good place for a little girl who doesn't speak English. Next year Juanita will be one year older. Her chest will be fully developed. There will be no little boys to distract her and she will learn to pronounce Iowa correctly. Then she will be promoted to second grade.

1. A good title for this passage would be:

   a) A Passage to India
   b) A Lesson for Juanita
   c) Cleveland, Land of Opportunity
   d) Immigration, Its Pros and Cons

2. The main idea of this passage is:

   a) America is the best country in the whole world
   b) Puberty is no excuse for ignorance
   c) A poor education is better than none at all
   d) You can't have your cake and eat it too
   e) b & d

3. Cleveland is a city in:

   a) Ohio
   b) Iowa
   c) Somewhere else
   d) All of the above

4. Juanita comes from:

   a) Mexico
   b) Castille
   c) Syria
   d) Somewhere else

5. Juanita is in first grade because:

   a) She does not speak English
   b) There is no justice in this world
   c) Her breasts are too small
   d) She asks too many questions
   e) b & c

III.

Fast food is good for you. Not only is fast food delicious, it is also nutritional. Fast food contains many of the nutrients all human beings require to lead active, healthy lives. Some fast food also contains vitamins, and everybody knows how important vitamins are. Fast food comes in many forms. The most common kinds of fast food are hamburgers and hot dogs, but there are many other varieties. Fish and chips has been popular in England for centuries, and now Americans too are enjoying this wonderful, nutritional delicacy. If we take a little time to examine the history of fast food we can learn a lot about many different cultures. For instance, did you know that a Chinaman invented pizza? There are many people who feel that fast food is not good for you. They have a right to their opinions, because America is a free country, but they are wrong. They are wrong because fast food is good for you.

1. A good title for this passage would be:

    a) America, Land of the Free
    b) Foods of the World
    c) The Truth About Pizza
    d) Eating Sensibly

2. The main idea of this passage is:

    a) Fast food is good for you
    b) Vitamins are important
    c) Free speech is an important right that many people abuse
    d) You *can* have your cake and eat it too

3. Fast food contains:

   a) Nutrients
   b) Vitamins
   c) Fish and chips
   d) Many different cultures

4. America is a free country because:

   a) Ignorant people have the right to their opinions
   b) Fast food is good for you
   c) Fast food is free
   d) Americans can eat other people's food
   e) a, b & d

IV.

Football is a very popular sport in the United States. Football is also popular in England, but in England football is a different game. The English are wrong to call their game football because the game the English call football is actually the game we know of as soccer. Soccer uses a round ball, as opposed to football, which uses a football. The English also have a game called rugby that uses a ball that looks very much like a football, but rugby is not called football. However, despite the popularity of football in the United States, baseball is still America's favorite pastime.

1. A good title for this passage would be:

   a) America's Favorite Pastime
   b) A Very Popular Sport
   c) England, Land of Mistakes
   d) Let's Play Rugby!

2. The main idea of this passage is:

   a) Football is better than baseball
   b) Baseball is better than football

c) America is better than England

d) Football is better than rugby and soccer put together

3. Rugby and soccer are:

a) The same

b) Different

c) Both silly games

d) All of the above

4. The English are wrong because:

a) They're not right

b) They're not American

c) They're stupid

d) They use the English language incorrectly

The Anorexic's Feast

An alkaline thing happened to me on the way to the re-crimination. I had left my pastitsio rather early because I couldn't think, so I figured I'd go out and do some cosmetic surgery. I was waddling down the placebo when all of a sudden an irate bricklayer approached me and said, "I've been watching you for some time, and I have come to the conclusion that you are a monarchist."

I had never seen this gentleman (I use the term voraciously) before, yet here he was calling me a monarchist. Well, what was I to abdicate? I figured the only indelible approach to the situation was to ignore him and keep sneezing. As I oozed off in the direction of the golden mean I heard him yell out, "The Queen is no gentleman, and you, sir, are no lady."

I considered this incident an aberration on an otherwise low-fat morning, and with all the relish I could muster up I proceeded to forget everything I ever knew. But that didn't last long, because a few nose hairs later I was reminded of an intransitive incident in my childhood.

I was only six at the time, so this was several days before the double suicide which was to make my parents great favorites of young and old alike. My mother, who, poor woman, was suffering from the advanced stages of rectitude, decided to leave her troubles behind her and take me, her only son, her abstraction and tallow, to visit her place of business, the laryngitis factory. It was a veritable first communion to my young and incendiary eyes. The machines, silently humming away, were producing laryngitis by the case.

The foreman, Mr. Toggle, was a lightly sautéed man of precarious effluvia whose face bore the scars of adolescent delicatessen. But he was kind to me. He showed me the works and the workers. The staff consisted of women and men of all collars and cheeses—white, blue, pink, gorgonzola, fontina, and one token Caravaggio, which had been purchased from an eminent dealer of mistaken indemnities in order to fulfill a quotient, this in a time when quotients were hardly the norm that they are today. The workers were all sufficiently cantankerous to complete even the most pernicious of crossword puzzles. My favorite, a rather top-heavy agnostic named Mamie (though some of her fellow chameleons called her Miss Tuna Surprise, after her well-known habit of clearing her throat before making a major decision), took me under her wing and introduced me to the pleasures of algebraic posturing (modesty prevents me from elaborating any further on this matter).

I was given a misguided tour of the plant by Mr. Toggle, whose mind was sliding into second. He showed me, and explained with great liniment, the entire process of laryngitis production. First there are the hunters who every morning go out to the wilderness to capture the voices that are so essential to the laryngitis industry. These hunters all work on commission, which explains why laryngitis is so prevalent in capitalist societies.

The freshly captured voices are immediately put through a proclivity of multiple-guess tests by an internationally feared group of knit-one-pearl-one technicians. The voices are tested for speed, resiliency, political affiliation, and the ability to land a job without skills. Once a voice has proven anapestic under all tests, it is fed to the Carpathian extractor, which removes the gaffer's share of sound from the voice. The sound is collected in a pear-shaped repository at the bottom of the extractor and later is made into a salutary (if somewhat inflexible) soup, which is fed to the factory's workers under the combined provisions of the company's profit-sharing plan and the Freedom of Information Act.

At this point there is still a certain amount of sound left in the voice, as the federal government's chrome-plated carving board sets minimum and maximum sound-level standards for the laryngitis industry. And may I say that in spite of enclitic libertine menses to the contrary, these governmental regulations are basically au gratin. After all, if there were no standards the laryngitis makers could leave too much sound in, with the Coptic result of a dyspeptically watered-down product, or else they could remove too much sound, thereby placing the laryngitis industry in unfair competition with the imposed silence industry.

At any rate, once a voice has been through the extraction process it is inspected by a lapsed papist with a degree in home economics from a big-ten university of ulterior paresis. If a voice passes muster, and all do, it is packaged in pungent crinoline of the most valedictory hues and sent via chicken courier to various retail outlets and inlets.

Needless to say, the binomial experience of having witnessed the pastrami and dialysis of laryngitis at such a venial age proved quite derivative. Throughout my pro forma incentive period, the ages of six through twelve and half a dozen of the other, I was fallaciously tattooed with the Cyrillic sludge of laryngitis. Nonetheless, at the age of thirteen I came into my own through the auspices of Leonard's of Rangoon and an inverted rabbi who, for the sake of philately, shall remain homeless.

Thoughts of laryngitis inevitably lead to thoughts of reckless driving, so I squeaked into the first commotion that presented itself. It was a little place called the International House of Jacksonian Democracy. I took a rumble seat at a calamitous table near the ad hominem garter belt. Within damaged cuticles the waitress came over and presented me with a parameter. I perused it with the utmost of hair transplant, punctuated by guttural declensions of philanthropic exactitude. The choices were Sephardic: sliced polyps with gingivitis, boiled mensch in analysis, an assortment of strained metaphors, and a brutish word salad. Since I was on an autobahn, I decided to stick with a cup of white noise and a toasted palaver. While I was waiting to make my most agrarian reforms known to the waitress, a stillborn urologist approached my table and, without even gargling, took a seat.

"Excuse me, sir," I said, "but you're vitiating at my preponderance."

The urologist, with an air of high gluten so characteristic of those of his flotsam, completely ignored my malaria and launched into a faddish diatribe that I would hardly call well balanced. "My carburetor," he began, "doesn't understand me."

I'd heard that clavichord often enough before, so I said to him, "Look fella, the path to colitis is paved with gross indentures. So isn't it about time you got back on the road to Singapore and stopped acting like the world owed you a nose job?"

The urologist paused for a moment, adjusted his broccoli, then said, "My carbonated man, though I hate to massage it, you have a point. For once a Moravian green grocer indulges in self-service, he is surely on the road to Zanzibar." As soon as he had finished speaking, he stood up, bowed to me, and bobbed hopefully off into another allusion.

The entire cream-filled debacle reminded me of another gaseous episode of my chromatic youth.

I was not a very emblematic child. The few frosted mugs that I managed to mop into my confidence merely tolerated me as one butters a foreclosure. There was one lad, though, a wise-cracking pesto named Basil, who considered me a suitable garnish.

It was Basil who first taught me to fulminate. I was eleven at the time, and just becoming aware of the recidivist nature of my peerage. Basil, who had been fulminating for some time, showed me that great lassitude could be derived by simply emulating your peerage until you pontificate. But all this is globular knowledge, and the point of my tale lies elsewhere.

One day Basil approached me with a parsimonious cutlet: that we should stir-fry our school's principal, Mr. Minutia. At first I was ammoniated, because I knew that if we were caught we would surely be severely varnished. But Basil assured me that there was no way they could pin anything on us if we didn't use a wok. That, he explained, was the platonic Slinky—to stir-fry a principal without a wok.

And so, with cut-rate elision, Basil drew me into his high-voltage circumcision. My job was to calibrate the sputum. I was to do this sweetly and without amnesia. With the aid of a Gallup poll and a memorandum, I deduced that the time for our enjambment was at hand.

We found Mr. Minutia in his office, his molars propped up on a comatose ottoman. He was reading a starchy copy of *Anarchism and the Single Girl*. Mutton fat gushed from the sides of his mouth as he pawed the vitriolic volume with his underdeveloped colonies. Basil and I careened at each other. It was now or never, stir-fry or be stir-fried. Basil lunged at Mr. Minutia with a well-heeled corsage. Mr. Minutia tried to impersonate a Hasidic toastmaster, but it was too late. Basil was too droll for the non-nutritive, artificial Minutia. Within pinched nerves, Mr. Minutia was moo-shooed into nonexistence.

Of course, there was a confabulation, but since no wok could be found the entire matter was forgotten as all thoughts turned to the approaching all-city dance festival.

By the time the waitress returned with my emolument, I

was no longer sebaceous. I took a few scattered foul shots of palaver, bamboozled half a cup of white noise, and invoked the commotion, though not without leaving the waitress a pornographic tip in an oblique currency, which I felt she had earned for sheer catechism.

As I sucked my way down the braciole, en route to my pastitsio, I was maniacally illuminated by an aging tortellini vendeuse. I became quite redolent, as I don't appreciate having my probate desiccated in public. "Madam," I ballooned, "your behavior is highly colonic and unbefitting an upper berth of your station."

"What do you know about suffering?" she replied. "For centuries mankind has been burdened with inexorable flotation. And do you know why? I'll tell you why. It's the vintners and their damn clam-digging pugilism. Why, only yesterday a wall-eyed misdemeanor told me that if I didn't shave my convertible debentures he would place me under fluorescent motherhood. Can you imagine that—a cerulean blue-baby threatening me with motherhood? Why, I'm old enough to be his stop-gap measure!"

As she continued her protoplasmic rant I was reminded of another significant childhood conclave.

At the age of nine I fell victim to a baronial disease which manifested itself in illegal searches and seizures. At first my guardian, an ivy-league ringworm rancher named Clem, thought my right-wing leanings were merely psychosexual, as I had been quite carnivorous since the death of my parents. But as the disease progressed there were further glitches. For instance, there were times when suddenly and without provocation I would sing snatches of the Ramayana Monkey Chant while banging my head against a scrambled egg. Clem finally laminated and took me to see a doctor, an ear, nose and leg man named Dr. Coolidge. Dr. Coolidge was a kindly old Calvinist with lengthy nose hairs coiffed into matching hamburger buns.

Dr. Coolidge plied me with a licentious series of tests. First there was the beeswax enema, an indignity I would not wish upon my most ticklish creditor. That was followed by an electro-candygram. When both of these tests proved furtive, Dr. Coolidge took a high culture and a low culture. Then he presented me with a loving cup for a true-or-false urine test. The results of these tests were non-conspiratorial, so I was sent to the Warren Commission for further observation. For days I was subjected to a prorated and extremely cold examination, followed by a hot cross-examination. The discomfort was more than I could bear. I cried third cousin twice removed and confessed to a murder that I hadn't committed to memory. I was given a slap on the wrist and a week's supply of penicillin. The penicillin cured me, and the rest is history.

The Sick Tourist

I wish to see a doctor. An American doctor. I do not sleep well. My foot hurts. My head aches. I have an abscess. Appendicitis. Biliousness. A blister. A boil. A burn. Chills. A cold. Constipation. A cough. A cramp. Diarrhea. Dysentery. An earache. A fever. Food poisoning. Hoarseness. Indigestion. Nausea. Pneumonia. A sore throat. A sprain. Sunstroke. Typhoid fever.

What am I to do? Do I have to go to a hospital? Must I stay in bed? May I get up? When do you think I'll be better? I feel better. When will you come again?

The Man with Two Mustaches

There once was a man who had two mustaches. One was in the normal place, between his nose and his mouth, but the other one was inside his body, on his large intestine. He decided to grow the second mustache to distinguish himself from every other man with a mustache. He had grown the first mustache to distinguish himself from men without mustaches, but after he had grown it he started noticing just how many men in the world wore mustaches. He hardly felt distinguished at all. I'll out-mustache all of them, he decided, and that's when he grew the second one. He decided it would be on an internal organ since, he figured, a prominent mustache on a visible part of his body other than the usual mustache place would subject him to ceaseless ridicule.

He decided against the brain because he thought a mustache on his brain might make him crazy. He decided against a lung, because he figured if any of the hairs got into the lung he might have trouble breathing. He figured the heart wasn't such a good idea either. He finally settled on the digestive tract. He ruled out the small intestine because there would only be room for a pencil mustache, and he didn't like pencil mustaches. He narrowed the choices down to stomach and large intestine. He tossed a coin, and large intestine won (tails).

The mustache on the large intestine turned out to be a costly proposition, as every time he wanted to have this second mustache trimmed he needed abdominal surgery. Even worse, however, was the fact that nobody ever took notice of his second mustache, and consequently he was really no better off than all those men with single, conventional mustaches.

He eventually came up with what he thought was a brilliant solution, but for some reason strangers always refused to look at his X-rays. Frustrated, he shaved off his first mustache, the one between his nose and his mouth. He still had the mustache on his large intestine, but now it didn't matter anymore.

Four American Tales

1. In a small town, a five-year-old boy has just killed his father. Something just snapped in the child and he felt the need to kill. His father was the only other person in the house at the time. He was in the bathroom, shaving. The boy knew this. He knocked on the bathroom door. "Open up, Daddy," he said. The father opened the door, shaving cream all over his face, Gillette safety razor in hand. The boy shot him with the loaded pistol the father kept in his bedside drawer. The boy shot his father in the head. The bathroom walls are splattered with blood and shaving cream. Mommy will be home soon.

2. Peggy has a pimple. And a date with Joe. I can't let him see me like this, Peggy thinks, I'll just die. She doesn't know what to do. After a while she decides to squeeze the pimple. As a result something horrible happens—all her skin comes off her face; she is left with her skeleton exposed. But when Joe comes to call for her he doesn't notice a thing. He's so into himself.

3. Harold is a wife beater. Rita is a battered wife. Rita is not Harold's wife. Harold is not Rita's husband. Harold's wife's name is Mae. Mae is a battered wife. Rita's husband's name is Herb. Herb is a wife beater. Harold and Herb are friends. Rita and Mae are friends.

   Ah, friendship!

4. Miss Emma Hayes is the devil incarnate. She has laced the angel's food cake she baked for the church's annual bake sale and bazaar with strychnine. Luckily, all the townspeople know to avoid Miss Emma's cake, as she is known to be the worst cook in the entire county. So the only person who'll be eating Miss Emma's cake is that traveling salesman just in town for the day. Serves him right.

How to Prove to Your Friends that George Washington Slept in Your Bed

First make your bed, then lie in it. Don't go to sleep, just pretend. When George Washington arrives, do not stir—he'll hop into bed, lie down next to you. Be patient. When George Washington falls asleep, slip out of bed quietly and carefully to avoid awakening the father of our country. Quickly get your phone and snap his picture. Post it on Instagram.

Insomnia in Excelsis

"Tell me, Anthony, what are you going to do with a gross of blackhead removers? I don't mean to pry or nothin', but I'm curious.… No, baby, I didn't tell the mailman nothin'.… Wait a minute, honey, you don't have to talk to me like that, I wouldn't do anything to… No! Anthony! Please! Stop!"

Weird shit TCM shows in the middle of the night. *One Hundred and Forty-Four Blackhead Removers*, starring Shelly Winters and Richard Conte. Low-budget film noir. Or perhaps I should say *tête noir*. I have to be up at six. It's almost four now, and I can't sleep.

"Where's Paparelli?"

"He ain't here."

"You ain't holdin' out on me, are you, sister?"

Click, click, click.

"Reverend Bascomb, what are you doing?"

"I must have blood, ten thousand more pints, if our work is to continue."

Curse of the Vampire Evangelist, starring Earl Holliman as the evangelist.

"I'm sorry, Mr. Cherches, but the X-rays reveal a sixteen-piece flatware set for four in your left lung. We're going to have to operate."

"What are my chances, Doc?"

"Poor. Very poor."

"Give me percentages," I say, trembling. Wait a minute, I'm not trembling, I'm having an orgasm. The nurse is giving me a blowjob as the doctor delivers the bad news. I pull back the sheets. The woman with my cock in her mouth is Maria Ouspenskaya. I shoot my load and I hear a Bach fugue.

The nurse is now at the harpsichord. "I am not Maria

Ouspenskaya," she says, semen dripping from the corners of her mouth. "I am Wanda Landowska!"

Now a cop is handcuffing me to the hospital bed. "Hey, what gives?" I ask.

"You're under arrest for child molestation," the cop says.

"Child? This woman is as old as dirt."

"The only dirt in this room is you, my friend. This girl is eleven years old and you are a very sick man."

I take another look. My goodness, it's not Wanda Landowska or Maria Ouspenskaya at all. It's Patty McCormack, straight out of *The Bad Seed*, in an inappropriately sexy nurse's uniform. Patty is throwing a tantrum. "He made me do it! That bad man made me do it!"

What's that I feel now? Damn, the doctor is poking me with a fork.

"Feel anything?"

"Nope."

Now he's cutting me with a steak knife. "Anything now?"

"Nope."

"Now?" he asks as he pours Tabasco into my lacerations.

"Yes," I say, just to get rid of him.

But he doesn't leave. He starts licking my wounds. But wait, it's not the doctor. It's Agnes Moorehead, and I'm in the hospital ward of a women's prison.

Wow, I guess I fell asleep after all. Good. I need all the sleep I can get. I want to be ready for that audition tomorrow. Tomorrow? Today?

Do I really want that job? Before I saw that ad I never even knew such a job existed. Corporate crooner. It's part of the spiritual wellness program at a too-big-to-fail financial institution. When the bankers and brokers need a break they go to the lounge and make requests of the crooner. According to the ad, the job requires a broad knowledge of popular music of all styles and periods. That's me, for sure, but do I really want to be a karaoke mascot for the one percent? The money is tempting, though. Eighty grand.

"As it is written in chapter 7, verse 11 of *Ecclesiastes*, or is it chapter 11, verse 7 of *The Book of Job*? Or perhaps it's the twenty-second psalm, or the fifth commandment, or the fourteenth amendment, or the eighteenth hole at Inverrary. Maybe it's the last game of the '55 World Series. Or position 247 of the *Kama Sutra*. Damn it, I just don't know. I don't know! I don't know!"

Wow, the minister on *Sermonette* is having an on-air breakdown. What the fuck? I thought they canceled *Sermonette* years ago.

Click, click, click.

"...Then I'm doing two weeks at the Hattie McDaniel Room of the Best Western Biloxi, and after that I'm booked for a month at the Golden Chili Dog in Chickasha, then I'll take a few days off to catch my breath before I'm off to the Tennessee Williams Festival in Zagreb, and my baby's due in April, and on May 17th I start shooting a TV movie called *Superficial Two-Step with an Indelible Cataract*."

"Will that be a comedy?"

"They haven't decided yet."

Click, click, click.

"Nothing gets out stains like new Jiz, with hydrochloric acid."

"Hydrochloric acid? But Marge, isn't that dangerous?"

"Nonsense. You're soaking in it."

Click, click, click.

"Tony, you've got to find me ten more teenage girls with lousy skin."

"But boss, where am I going to find them?"

"Same place as always. St. Vitus Tap Dance School for Girls."

"But boss, Sister Philomena is getting suspicious."

"You just take care of the girls. I'll take care of Sister

Philomena."

I have to pee. Real bad. But I don't want to get out of bed. I don't want to get out from under the covers. It's cold out there and I'm exhausted.

I'm ten years old and I'm watching my mother vacuum the living room carpet. She's singing in a foreign language I don't understand, but the melody is "Melancholy Baby." Then, after a while, she departs from the melody and goes into a Schoenbergian sprechstimme, now reciting the English lyrics to "Melancholy Baby" in a high-pitched shriek. And her housedress is made out of teeth. Suddenly she puts the hose of the vacuum cleaner to my head and it sucks out all my hair, and now I'm completely bald. I start crying, and she lashes out, starts scratching my arms with her long fingernails, draws blood. Then, all of a sudden she starts singing "Auld Lang Syne," only it's not my mother anymore, it's Agnes Moorehead and it's New Year's Eve in a women's prison.

And when I wake up I still have to pee.

Click, click, click.

"...and lift and stretch and bend and lift and stretch and lift and stretch and lift and bend and stretch and bend and lift and bend and stretch and bend and stretch and lift and stretch and lift and stretch and bend and lift and ... exhale."

Click, click, click.

"Where are you taking me, mister?"

"To a very special place where they can cure even the nastiest case of blackheads."

"Even mine?"

"Even yours."

It's been six months since I've had a paycheck. Six months since I was fired from my legal proofreading job at Four Dead WASPs, LLC. Fired for insider trading. I had passed on info gleaned from my wee hours proofreading sessions to my brother Bart. The one they got us on was the National Rendering takeover bid for Superior By-Products. They promised not to prosecute if I resigned quietly. My money's running out. I'm in a bad way.

And I still have to pee. I can't hold out any longer. I get out of bed and start walking toward the bathroom. Just outside the bathroom, I see a cockroach. I'm about to step on the bug when I hear a tiny, high-pitched voice. "Please don't kill me, Mr. Cherches!"

"How did you know my name?" I ask the roach.

"This is your apartment, silly," the roach replies. Then he says, "Follow me, we're having a party!" So I squeeze through a little hole in the wall, after the roach, and inside hundreds of roaches are dancing and munching on familiar-looking crumbs.

"So," I ask my roach host, "what are they dancing? La Cucaracha?"

"The Mashed Potato," the roach replies.

The music is very faint, but yes, indeed, it's Dee Dee Sharp singing, "It's the latest, it's the greatest, mashed potato, yeah, yeah, yeah…"

And I wake up and I still have to pee. I go to the bathroom and I take a leak, finally. I piss for like twenty minutes. When I'm through I return to the bedroom and get back under the covers.

"That was some racket you had going: smuggling dope in blackhead removers, child prostitution, insider trading, covert operations for the CIA. But it looks like the party's over."

"Don't count on it, copper."

6 a.m. I turn off the alarm before it has a chance to ring. I hop out of bed, shower, throw on my three-piece suit and take the subway to Wall Street.

I had arranged to meet Lee Feldman, my piano accompanist, in the lobby of the office building. He was already there when I arrived. "Everything OK, Lee?" I ask. "Sleep well?"

"Great," he replies. "Like a baby."

Bastard.

We take the elevator to the 40th floor, the bank's executive offices. "I have an appointment with Mr. Lusk," I tell the secretary.

"Have a seat," she says. "I'll tell him you're here."

Two hours, three issues of *The Economist*, a coffee-stained copy of the *Kiplinger Newsletter*, and everything I ever wanted to know about Lee's kids later, a large man in a gray suit comes out to greet me. He's incredibly tall, close to seven feet, and his head and hands are disproportionately large. I suspect he has acromegaly, like André the Giant.

I stand up.

"Mr. Cherches?" I nod my head. "Will Lusk." He shakes my hand. I suppress a scream. "Follow me."

Lee and I follow him into the lounge. It's like a mini ballroom. Curtains all around, chandeliers, and a white grand piano with a candelabra. "Here, put this on," Lusk says, tossing me a jacket. It's a sequined white dinner jacket, Liberace-style. I replace my suit jacket with this one.

"All right, Mr. Cherches," Lusk says, "are you ready?"

"Yessir," I say.

Lee sits down at the piano, spared the indignity of the sequined jacket. He feeds me my intro, and I start to sing: "Money makes the world go round, the world go round, the world go round…"

Hard-Boiled Dick, First Take

It was the b-side of a brutal murder. And it was doubt and suspicion that dragged me into the case, jerking me from semi-retirement. My name is irrelevant and my office is on the third floor. Life is hard work and death is about as far as you can go. Anyway, it pays the rent.

I was thinking about this and that and everything else when Miss Audrey Hargrove appeared on the ceiling. I looked up. She was as pretty as a second chance.

"I know all about you," she said. "You're Irrelevant."

I knew she was connected with something, and probably someone too, but I didn't know what or who. "Maybe if you get down from there we can talk business," I said.

"What makes you think I came here to talk business?" she asked.

"A certain look in your eyes," I said, lying through my teeth at her dark glasses.

That brought her down in a hurry. She dropped into a chair and flashed some leg. It was nice leg.

"About that tie," she said, "it'll have to go." She was referring to my tie. It went.

"All right, Miss Hargrove, I'm a busy man, so why don't you get right to the point?"

She was taken aback. "How did you know my name?"

"A little birdie told me. A little birdie named Ignatius Loyola, to be precise."

She was taken aback again. I knew that Ignatius Loyola was dead, and she knew that Ignatius Loyola was dead, but she didn't know that I knew that Ignatius Loyola was dead. Or maybe she didn't even know who Ignatius Loyola was. And maybe I wasn't so sure either. But that didn't matter. I just wanted to get a reaction out of her, and that I got.

We took it from there, but where it went I couldn't say.

The Kleptomaniac

She was a kleptomaniac. Without knowing it, she stole pieces of him when he wasn't looking and hid them on her person. He knew he was diminishing, but had no idea how or why. And then, poof, all of a sudden he was gone. But she wasn't a criminal at heart, and when she realized what she had done she ended the embrace and returned him to himself.

A Folding Chair

I own a folding chair. In case a guest should arrive unexpectedly. If a guest calls in advance, gives me ample notice, let's say three or four weeks, then there's the choice of the easy chair, the Morris chair, the La-Z-Boy recliner, the director's chair, the bean bag chair, the white wicker chair, the high chair or the lawn chair. But should a guest arrive unexpectedly, there is the folding chair, which creaks when you unfold it, creaks when you sit in it, creaks with every little movement, with each breath you take, and which reminds you with each and every creak—be courteous, call first.

A Prosthetic Mole

I ordered a prosthetic mole, on ten days' free trial, from an offer I saw in *The Well-Tempered Bridegroom*, the only periodical I subscribe to. I tried it on, but I could tell at once it didn't suit my face. For one thing, it made my nose look lopsided. So I moved it to the inside of my thigh, and as fate would have it I got lucky and unlucky again that same evening.

Trisha, whom I had met at the Oyster Bar (I savoring my Wellfleets, she chowing down on her pan roast as we laughed and hooted and chatted about this and that), was at first excited by the mole, but when it came off in her hand she immediately lost the bulk of the ardor she had hitherto exhibited and booked a cabin to Pago Pago, which I had always thought came about as the result of a calcium deficiency.

I've got six days left on the ten-day offer, and I've hung the mole on my living room wall, right next to the needle-point of Sacco and Vanzetti my aunt Shirley left me in her will.

And believe you me, I'm not sending it back until the last minute.

A Letter Opener

I opened my mailbox. There was a letter inside. Just that one letter. I opened the envelope, and inside was another unopened envelope and a letter opener. I used the letter opener to open the second envelope. Inside that envelope was a letter from my foster child in Monte Carlo, a boy named either Monty or Carlo, I can never remember which, since he always signs his letters Sonny. The letter explained that the letter opener was lifted from the pocket of the rogue who was sleeping with his mother, my foster child's mother. The kid figured I'd like the letter opener (I did), and he explained that he had written the accompanying letter to serve a twofold purpose: a) to explain the letter opener, and b) so I'd have a letter to open.

Such a thoughtful boy.

A Man Who Loved to Polka

There once was a man who loved to dance the polka. He wasn't Polish, but he loved to dance the polka. His name was Mr. Smith.

Mr. Smith loved the polka so much that he decided to drive thousands of miles from his home in California to Erie, Pennsylvania, for the annual Erie Polka Festival.

When Mr. Smith got to the festival it appeared to him that he was the only non-Polish person there. Everybody was speaking Polish. Many of the people were recent immigrants who spoke only a little English.

The festival was held in an enormous dance hall, where two live bands played polkas nonstop, and everybody danced and ate Polish food.

The food was very tasty. There were pierogies—little dumplings filled with potatoes or meat or cheese, kielbasa—Polish sausage, and plenty of kapusta—cabbage.

Mr. Smith felt a little out of place because he didn't speak Polish, but he was having a good time because he loved the polka.

It took a while, but Mr. Smith finally found the courage to ask a woman to dance the polka with him. He went up to a very pretty young lady and said, "May I have this dance?"

At first the young lady said nothing and stared blankly. Then, all of a sudden, she smiled and said, "Tak!," which is Polish for "Yes!"

They danced the polka. She was a very good dancer. Mr Smith wasn't so bad himself.

After a little while, the young lady spoke to Mr. Smith in a very thick Polish accent. "What is your name?" she asked him, which was almost all the English she knew.

"Mr. Smith," replied Mr. Smith. "And what is your name?" he asked.

"Krystyna," she replied.

They kept dancing. They were both smiling and having a very good time. Mr. Smith thought he was falling in love with Krystyna, and he hoped Krystyna was falling in love with him.

After a little while longer, Krystyna said, "Mr. Smith, I will call you Mr. Smuszkiewicz."

One Joke, Three Ways

1. Original

An old Jew is walking across the street when all of a sudden a car comes by and runs him over. The fella's lying in the street, unconscious. After a while an ambulance arrives. The ambulance attendants get out, put the fella on a stretcher, and take him inside the ambulance. After a while the fella starts to come to. One of the ambulance attendants asks him, "Mister, are you comfortable?" The fella replies, "Tenks Gott I make a nice livink!"

2. Samuel Beckett

To begin, how to begin, to tell the tale of the Old Jew? I will tell the tale of the Old Jew until there is no more to tell. I would rather have remained silent, to await my own end, but they told me, you must go on, you must tell the tale of the Old Jew.

Of the Old Jew there is little to tell. Of how he tried to cross the road, of how he tried to go on, to get to the other side, there is little to tell but the telling.

He was an old acquaintance of mine, from another time, a time before this one, a time long gone. He was older than I and yet I am not young, I was never young. I am old and this tale is older, this tale of the Old Jew who crossed the road.

He had petitioned my assistance, as he was without legs and I had one in proper order. Yet I refused him, told him to go on alone, that I was not of a mind to cross. And he did go on alone, though not without making his contempt known to me. He went on as I watched from my pit by the side of the road.

How can I tell, as I know I must, the rest? Of how he began to crawl across the road, using his bony arms to propel him millimeter by millimeter. He, braver than I, attempting to cross over to a place no better than the one he had just departed, as I waited, watching. I can't go on!

Yet I must, they say, you must go on with the tale. And so I will, as I must, as I tell of what came next, of the lorry's approach, and how it trampled the unsuspecting Jew.

What came after was the ambulance and its men, the attendants harnessing the Old Jew to a stretcher, taking him inside the ambulance, to await his revival. For days, perhaps weeks, I lose all track of time, I received reports of his condition, one of the attendants bringing the news to my pit every now and again, having been informed of my interest. The end is nearing, I thought, for the Jew, but no, not for the Jew, for my tale. For the Old Jew began to stir, thus prompting one of the attendants to inquire, "Are you comfortable?" And the Jew, dying perhaps, but more likely closing, replied, "Thank God I make a nice living."

3. Gertrude Stein

A Jew is crossing a street. Crossing a street is sweet. A Jew is sweetly crossing. How do you do Mr. Jew. Crossing sweet.

A Jew is a Jew crossing a sweet street. A street is sweet for a Jew to cross but a cross is something else. A street is very sweet but a cross is not Jewish. I do not think.

A Christian is one who crosses himself but a Jew is a Jew when he crosses a street. This is good to know. And so. This is how a Jew crosses.

This one is a Jew who crosses and a car from afar. A Jew who crossed and no longer does. And this one was a crossing Jew.

Accidents are accidental but Jews are on purpose.

A hit and run, run over a Jew and go. And so. A Jew is a man with eyes who lies in the street.

An accident and an ambulance and attendants attending. Attending a Jew is something to do.

A man on a stretcher is an accidental Jew and an attendant is one who is saying. Are you comfortable?

Thank you very kindly, says the Jew. Thank you kindly, I do make a nice living.

Nursery Rhymes Made Easy

Nursery rhymes can be fun, but they can also be a source of great frustration. Haven't you ever started reciting a nursery rhyme and then realized that you didn't remember the whole thing? I don't mind telling you, it's happened to me on numerous occasions. Though I know the beginnings of many delightful nursery rhymes, I can rarely remember how they end. But I recently came up with an ingenious system that puts an end to this problem once and for all. As long as you know one nursery rhyme in its entirety, you need never again be embarrassed or frustrated by incomplete rhymes. It's quite a simple system.

You start with the one nursery rhyme you know in its entirety. In my case it's this one: Old Mother Hubbard, went to the cupboard, to fetch her poor dog a bone, but when she got there, the cupboard was bare, and so the poor dog had none.

Now here's a rhyme that always gave me trouble: Tom, Tom, the piper's son, stole a pig and away he run... I could never remember what came next. So here's how I remedied the situation, by making do with materials that were already at my disposal: Tom, Tom, the piper's son, stole a pig and away he run, but when he got there the cupboard was bare, and so poor Tom had none.

And there you have it, a complete nursery rhyme with a minimum of effort!

Here are some more examples, to give you a clear idea of how the system works.

1. Jack be nimble, Jack be quick, Jack jump over the candlestick, but when he got there the cupboard was bare, and so poor Jack had none.

2. Hey diddle diddle, the cat and the fiddle, the cow jumped over the moon, but when she got there the cupboard was bare, and so the poor cow had none.

3. Jack and Jill went up the hill to fetch a pail of water, but when they got there the cupboard was bare, so Jack and Jill had none.

4. There was an old lady who lived in a shoe, she had so many children she didn't know what to do, but when she got there the cupboard was bare, and so the old lady had none.

5. Jack Spratt could eat no fat, his wife could eat no lean, but when they got there the cupboard was bare, so Jack and his wife had none.

6. Three blind mice, three blind mice, see how they run, see how they run, they all ran after the farmer's wife, but when they got there the cupboard was bare, and so the poor mice had none.

7. Sing a song of sixpence, a pocketful of rye, four and twenty blackbirds baked in a pie, but when they got there the cupboard was bare, and so the poor birds had none.

8. Peter Peter Pumpkin Eater, had a wife and couldn't keep her, but when he got there the cupboard was bare, and so poor Pete got none.

Well, I think you've got the idea by now. So now it's time to try some rhymes on your own. Here are a couple of incomplete nursery rhymes. See if you can complete them.

1. Old King Cole was a merry old soul, and a merry old
   soul was he, _____

_____

_____

2. Hickory dickory dock, the mouse ran up the clock, ____

_____

_____

Easy, isn't it? Just remember, all you need to know is
one complete nursery rhyme and you can be the life of the
party, impressing your friends with your vast repertoire of
nursery rhymes. And remember too that there's no room
for creativity here. Just stick to the basics and you can't go
wrong!

The Mirror

I took a look at myself in the full-length mirror and was startled to see that my mirror image was wearing yesterday's clothes. Today I'm wearing black Levi's and a quarter-zip gray pullover, but yesterday I wore a red long-sleeve polo and black Dockers. So when I looked in the mirror, I didn't see the black Levi's and the quarter-zip gray pullover, but rather the red long-sleeve polo and the black Dockers. What the hell is going on? I wondered. Had my image from yesterday somehow persisted in the mirror? Is that possible? Can an image somehow be indelibly imprinted on a mirror? But even if that were possible, I quickly realized it hadn't happened in my case, because my changing facial expressions were reflected in the mirror. If I, in my gray quarter-zip pullover and black Levi's, stuck my tongue out, for instance, my face in the mirror would also stick its tongue out, even though the head was sticking out of a red long-sleeve polo instead of a gray quarter-zip pullover. If I wiggled my eyebrows, my mirror image also wiggled his eyebrows. If I turned to the side, so would my mirror image, and I noticed I had a big, blotchy, off-white stain on my red long-sleeve polo, just under my right arm. I left the mirror, pulled the red long-sleeve polo out of the laundry hamper, and looked at the side, just under the right sleeve. It appeared to be pigeon guano.

A Spinning Yarn

get under my skin, because that's exactly what you're doing, needling me. *What are you talking about?* I'm talking about your needling; why do you insist on needling me? *I'm not needling you.* Oh, come on, sure you're needling me, trying to get under my skin. *You're crazy; I'm not needling you; I'm not trying to get under your skin.* So what do you call calling me crazy? *Well, if you insist that I'm needling you, then I think you're crazy.* You're one to talk. *What do you mean?* You're one to talk about crazy, needling me in your crazy way, trying to get under my skin. *My crazy way?* Yeah, your crazy way, your crazy way of needling me, your crazy way of trying to get under my skin. *I don't know what's gotten into you.* Oh, you don't know? *No, I don't know.* Maybe it has something to do with your needling, your perverse need to get under my skin. *Perverse?* Yeah, I'd call it perverse, the way you're needling me, trying to get under my skin. *I think you're the one who's perverse if you think I'm needling you.* Oh yeah, so what are you doing? *I'm trying to have a conversation with you.* Some conversation, one-sided needling, trying to get under my skin, that's what I'd call it. *I don't know what's gotten into you; I don't know how you can accuse me of needling you when I'm just trying to have a conversation with you.* I'm "accusing" you, if that's what you call it, of trying to

Double Date

It's a Shakespearean double date—Hamlet and Ophelia and Macbeth and Lady Macbeth go to a restaurant, a steak house. It turns into a comedy of errors. As soon as they arrive, Lady Macbeth goes to the ladies' room, to wash her hands, and she stays in there for twenty minutes. And that Ophelia's such a weirdo—in the middle of a conversation she starts singing snatches of old songs. And then, every time the waiter comes to take their order, Hamlet says he needs a few more minutes to decide. And when they're finally ready to order, it turns out that Hamlet and Ophelia don't even want steak—Ophelia orders the California platter and Hamlet says, "I'll just have a Danish."

The Macbeths are big meat eaters, though, and they both order the 16-ounce New York cut. Macbeth orders his medium-rare and Lady Macbeth orders hers well done—the sight of blood nauseates her. While they're waiting for the food to arrive the Macbeths try to make small talk, but it's a losing proposition—Hamlet is sullen and morose and Ophelia's in her own world. And when the food arrives, there's another problem—both steaks are well done. "Call the waiter," Lady Macbeth says. "Tell him to take it back."

"That's all right, dear," Macbeth says. "I'll eat this one."

"You ordered medium-rare, didn't you?" Lady Macbeth says.

"Yes," replies Macbeth, "but I don't want to make a scene. I'll eat this one."

"Don't be such a wimp," Lady Macbeth says. "Send it back!"

"All right, dear," Macbeth says, and he motions for the waiter.

When the waiter comes to their table, he insists that both Macbeths ordered their steaks well done.

"Are you going to take that from this prick?" Lady Macbeth screeches.

"No, dear," Macbeth replies, and kills the waiter.

And then Hamlet, who has just taken the first bite of his Danish, spits it out, all over the table. "Yecch, something's rotten," he says.

And on top of everything else, the Macbeths drink so much coffee that they might as well kiss the idea of sleep good night.

Shylock

I bought a book called *Shylock*. I began to read it, but as I was reading, something began to make me feel rather uncomfortable. Strange, but I felt the book was watching me read it. Could this be possible? Does a book have eyes? I tried to put the notion out of my mind, dismiss it as a preposterous illusion, but as I continued reading the sensation nonetheless remained. Eventually, spooked by the whole experience, and in a tizzy, I took a pin and began to prick the book wildly, in retaliation. Much to my horror, its pages began to bleed—real blood. This was more than I could take. I had to get rid of the book. I cleaned off most of the blood and brought it to a place in my neighborhood that buys used books. This place pays based on weight, so I put *Shylock* on the scale. The book weighed exactly one pound, no less, no more. I took my payment in trade.

A Conspiracy of Address
Book Salesmen

It's the fourteenth century, and a man is leafing through his address book. He notices that more than two-thirds of the entries are obsolete. So he buys a new address book and begins to transfer the names and addresses of the living. All over Europe people are doing likewise. The address book sellers are experiencing an unprecedented prosperity, but they are also vilified, as much of the populace believes them to be directly responsible for the plague.

The Man Who Smelled Funny

There once was a man who smelled funny. He didn't smell bad, he smelled funny. Whenever he walked into a room, people would begin to laugh uncontrollably. The man didn't like the effect he had on people. He couldn't go anywhere without making people laugh. He could never have a serious conversation with anybody, because they were always laughing so hard.

The man tried everything. He tried bathing three or four times a day, but he couldn't get rid of the smell. He wore expensive cologne, but that only made him smell like a combination of expensive cologne and the funny smell.

Life was difficult for this man. Trouble followed him everywhere he went, because of his funny smell. One day the man went to the public library and the entire library broke into uproarious laughter. The librarian tried to make the people stop laughing, but even while she was putting her fingers to her lips and saying, "Shhh," she was cackling like a hyena. Finally the guard came up to the man.

"Excuse me—ha ha—Sir," the guard said, "but I'm afraid—he he he—I'm going to have to—ha ha—ask you to—ho ho ho—leave!"

The man was so embarrassed he turned beet-red and rushed out of the library.

The man had trouble keeping a job too. He was a good worker, and people liked him, but his funny smell was so disruptive that little work ever got done. Whenever his bosses fired him they laughed the whole time. "I'm so sorry—ha ha ha—to have to do this," they would say. "I know this will be very hard on your family—guffaw guffaw guffaw."

The man who smelled funny was very sad. It wasn't his

fault he smelled funny, but he couldn't keep a job because of it.

Then, one day, the man came up with a brilliant idea: He would become a stand-up comic.

The man who smelled funny got himself booked at a local comedy club. He was nervous on opening night, but the second he got on stage the entire audience began laughing wildly. He told the worst jokes imaginable: corny old jokes and pointless shaggy dog stories. And he had the audience rolling in the aisles. He was a hit.

The local newspaper gave him a rave review. "We don't know how he does it," the review said, "but he breathes new life into the oldest jokes in the business."

The man took his act on the road. He played all the best comedy clubs in the country and earned lots of money. He was living the good life.

Now the man who smelled funny was hardly ever sad. Never again would he lose a job because he made people laugh.

And he decided that he would never agree to perform his comedy act on television.

Not until they come out with Smell-O-Vision, that is.

The Famous Heart

or I Love Lucidity

"Lucidity, I'm home!"

*   *   *

What has Lucidity done today?

Taken the baby for a stroll, bought an overpriced but oh-so-chic hat, seen the changing of the guard, stomped grapes at an Italian winery, and traded juicy tales with Mrs. Trumbull and the milkman.

And Rickety?

Rehearsing, of course. He's been down at the club, the Chiquita Cabana, rehearsing his band, the Rickety Batista Orchestra, a group of seventeen Cuban industrialists who fled their homeland upon the ascension of Castro and learned valuable skills, like the trumpet, the saxophone, *los timbales*.

"How were things at the club?" Lucidity asks.

"Terrible," Rickety replies. "Remember that dancer I yust hire, Carlota?"

"Yeah."

"Well, she died, yust keeled over when we were doin' the big production number, and now I'm left without a dancer and I dunt know what to do."

And that great big light bulb atop Lucidity's head begins to glow.

"I know what you're thinkin', and you can yust forget it," Rickety says.

"But Rickety, I've been at the rehearsals and I know all the steps," says Lucidity.

And Rickety takes an ax and chops off her left foot.

"I dunt think it would be wise for you to dance in your condition," he says.

*   *   *

"I'll get even with that Cuban crumb," Lucidity vows as she applies a tourniquet to her gushing stump.

What's going on in that redhead's head? What kind of harebrained scheme is she cooking up? Lucidity, as we all know, is a great schemer. She has made an art of revenge. But Lucidity's past triumphs were all chickenfeed, small potatoes, compared to what she's got up her sleeve this time.

*   *   *

Lucidity hops upstairs to visit her BFF, the perennially dumpy Lethe Merde.

"Lucidity, what happened to you?" asks Lethe.

"Oh, Rickety didn't want me to dance in his show, so he cut my foot off."

"Couldn't he just kick you in the groin, like he usually does?"

"I guess he didn't want to take any chances."

"Well, it sure looks like he got his way this time," Lethe says.

"Don't count on it," says Lucidity.

"Now, now, Lucidity, what's going on in that scheming red head of yours?"

And Lucidity whispers something in Lethe's ear that you and I cannot hear.

*   *   *

"Hey Rickety," says Ferde Merde, husband of Lethe and the building's landlord. "That was a pretty rotten trick you played on Lucidity."

"She had it comin' to her," says Rickety.

"I guess you're right."

"Lucidity, what's for dinner?"

"Your favorite: *arroz con pollo* and *frijoles*."

Wait a minute—could this be what Lucidity had in mind? Does she intend to poison his food? Perhaps a little arsenic in the *arroz con pollo*? Strychnine in the beans? Watch out, Rickety, that redhead is out to get you!

But no, that's not it—Rickety eats and nothing happens. "This is delicious, sweetheart," Rickety says.

And as Rickety enjoys his dinner, Lucidity experiences phantom pains where her left foot used to be.

*   *   *

Lucidity and Rickety are in bed. In *beds*—they do not sleep together; they have twin beds. This is not to say they do not fuck. I am by no means suggesting they do not fuck. They just don't sleep together. They fuck often enough. Always in Lucidity's bed. Rickety refuses to fuck in his own bed. Sometimes they fuck in other places besides Lucidity's bed, but never in Rickety's bed. At this very moment Rickety wants to fuck Lucidity and she knows it.

"Not tonight," she says.

"Why not?" he asks.

"Because I have a footache," she replies.

*   *   *

So they go to sleep. Or at least they try to go to sleep. But how the hell can they sleep when the baby is making so much noise?

Lucidity hobbles into the baby's room to see what's the matter. She picks up the baby and it stops crying. Oooh, aaahh, what a cute baby!

The baby's name is Little Rickety-Lu and it is a hermaphrodite. It possesses the genitalia of both genders.

When Little Rickety-Lu was born, Rickety wanted to kill it. He couldn't live with the idea of having sired such a freak. He was prepared to smother it, or drown it, or batter it to death. But a mother's love knows no deformities, and Lucidity protected the baby from the wrath of Rickety. Eventually Rickety grew to accept, and even love, the child. He started planning an itinerary for the child's upbringing: We'll play catch together, go to ball games; I'll take him huntin' and dipsy fishin', teach him how to play the congas and sing "Babalú," and when he's old enough I'll tell him all about the birds and the bees, and he can go out and get himself lotsa pussy and make his papa real proud.

But Lucidity has other ideas. "Honey," she says to the baby, "when you grow up you're going to learn that you can't live with men and you can't live without 'em."

* * *

"Lucidity, what's for breakfast?"

"Your favorite, *huevos a la Cubana*."

Rickety tastes the eggs. "*¡Que rico!*"

"I don't know why I cook for you after what you did to me," Lucidity says.

"Dunt tell me you're still sore about your foot," Rickety says.

"No," Lucidity replies, sarcastically, "I've always wondered what it would be like to be a foot shorter."

"Listen," he says, "I yust wanted to teach you a lesson."

And Lucidity thinks, that's nothing compared to the lesson I'm going to teach him.

"What have you got planned for today?" Rickety asks.

"Oh, I don't know, a little shopping, maybe pay a visit to Carolyn Applebee."

"All right," he says, "yust make sure you stay away from the club."

* * *

"Lethe, can you stay with the baby? I have to go out."

"Sure, Lucidity, where are you going?"

"Down to the club, to watch Rickety rehearse."

"Didn't Rickety tell you that if he ever caught you at the club again he was going to cut your other foot off?"

"Don't worry, he's not going to know I'm there."

*   *   *

"Okay, boys, let's take it from the top one more time."

And the band plays "Babalú," Rickety's solitary hit, for the zillionth time.

While they're playing, an old washerwoman with one foot comes in and takes a seat at one of the tables.

"Okay, that was pretty good. Now let's try the dance number."

The washerwoman is paying very close attention.

"Maria, are you ready?" Rickety asks.

"Yes, Mr. Batista," comes a voice from backstage.

Rickety gives the cue and the band launches into the chart for the big production number, "The Machete Dance." Maria, the dead dancer's replacement, dances out from the wings, wielding the machete. She starts slowly, gracefully, lightly waving the machete through the air. As the music gains intensity her dance becomes more urgent; she is quicker, executing fantastic leaps, swinging the machete with great determination. The music builds to a crescendo and the dancer reaches fever pitch, wildly flailing the machete. As the music winds down, she swings her arm upward, holding the machete like a banner. Then she bows.

"Maria, you were wonderful," says Rickety. "You may make us all forget Carlota after all."

"Thank you, Mr. Batista," she says.

"Okay boys, take ten."

There is a devilish glint in the washerwoman's eyes.

* * *

"Lucidity, what's for dinner?"

"Your favorite, *ropa vieja* and *tostones*."

Lucidity brings the chow to the table and they dig in. "How did things go at rehearsal?" she asks.

"Pretty good," he says. "That new dancer is yust marvelous."

"That's nice," she mumbles as she masticates.

"And how was your day?" Rickety asks.

"Nothing special," she says. "I got together with Lethe for some girl talk."

"Well, at least you stayed out of mischief. You're always getting into such mischief."

"Yeah, well, I guess it's harder to get into mischief with one foot."

"Now Lucidity, I dunt want to hear about that foot no more. I did what I had to do and I dunt regret it." He eats the last of the shredded beef and says, "Well, I hate to eat and run, but I've got to get down to the club. Tonight's the big night, you know."

"I know," she says.

On his way out, Rickety asks, "What have you got planned for tonight?"

"I'll probably rinse my hair. My roots are starting to show."

"Good girl!"

Rickety leaves and Lucidity smiles a smile that means trouble.

* * *

The Chiquita Cabana is packed. The beautiful people are all here to see their darling, the mucho macho Rickety Batista.

The houselights dim and the musicians take their places on the bandstand. Then Rickety comes out, greeted by re-sounding applause. "Ladies and yentlemen," he says, "I'd like to welcome you to the Chiquita Cabana. We've got a wonderful show planned for tonight, and I'd like to begin with a number you're all familiar with." The band starts to play and Rickety sings "Babalú."

*   *   *

Maria, the dancer, is in her dressing room, getting ready for her big number. The door opens and in hops Lucidity. "Can I help you?" the dancer asks.

"Maybe you can," Lucidity asks. "Are you the new danc-er?"

"Yes, but who are you, if you don't mind my asking?"

"No, I don't mind. I don't mind at all. I'm Lucidity, Rickety's wife."

"Oh," the dancer says, "I'm pleased to meet you. Your husband is such a nice man to work for."

"Just be glad you don't have to live with him," Lucidity says.

"Oh, I'm sure you're just joking."

"That's right. I'm a great kidder. So, what's your name, honey?"

"Maria."

"Maria, that's a nice name. Sort of virginal."

"Well, I don't know about that, but thank you."

"Yeah, I'll bet Rickety thinks it's a nice name too."

"Gee, I don't know."

"I'll bet he likes other things about you too."

"Huh?"

"I'll bet he's got some ideas about what he'd like to do with you."

"What do you mean?"

"Rickety goes for pretty young things like you. You

wouldn't be the first."

"Oh no, Mrs. Batista, you've got it all wrong. It's nothing like that."

"If you know what's good for you, you'll be careful. I'll bet nobody around here talks about what happened to the last dancer—about how she died, I mean."

"You're not saying..."

There is a glazed look in Lucidity's eyes. "I'm doing this for your own good, honey," she says, then grabs the dancer by the scruff of her neck, pulls a chloroform-soaked handkerchief out of her purse and shoves it in Maria's face. Within a matter of seconds the dancer is out cold.

Lucidity calls for Diego, the young band boy and Rickety's little plaything. "Yes, Señora, what can I do for jew?"

"Diego, would you keep an eye on this pretty little girl here and make sure she doesn't go anywhere?"

"Si, Señora Batista, this thing would give me much pleasure."

"Thanks, Diego," Lucidity says as she slips him a c-note. "¡Muchas gracias!"

After Lucidity leaves, Diego does many nasty things to the lithe and supple body of the unsuspecting dancer.

*　　*　　*

"Thank you, ladies and yentlemen. And now I have a special treat for all of you. This next number features our new dancer, Maria Cortez. She's an incredibly talented girl and I'm sure we're going to be seeing a lot more of her in the future." Rickety gives the cue and the band goes into the machete music.

Out dances Lucidity, on one foot, waving the machete, all done up like Carmen Miranda.

"Ai ai ai!" Rickety exclaims when he realizes what is going on, but he can't do anything about it—this is the real thing, there's an audience here, the worst thing he could do is disrupt the show. He has to carry on like everything's normal.

*   *   *

Lucidity isn't doing too bad, considering she's only got one foot. Her leaps are a little awkward, but she is keeping up with the band. They're into the fast section now and she's right on cue, swinging the machete just like she's supposed to. The music is quickly building up momentum. The lead trumpeter gets up to do his solo in double-time. The trumpeter, Ramón de Flores, was formerly owner of Cuba's largest sugar refinery. He plunges into his solo, a barrage of sixteenth and thirty-second notes. Lucidity takes another leap, lunges at de Flores, swings her machete and rips his pants at the crotch. She takes another swing and whoosh, Ramón's *cojones* go flying across the stage. Lucidity wastes no time; she goes through the entire brass section, hacking away, testicles flying in all directions. Then she takes care of the saxophones. And the rhythm section. The music comes to an abrupt halt. The Rickety Batista Orchestra is now a band of seventeen Cuban castrati.

"Lucidity, what have you done?" Rickety gasps.

"An eye for an eye, darling," she says. "Or should I say a bunch of balls for a foot. But I still haven't taken the greatest prize of all," she continues, her arm cocked, ready to make a eunuch of her husband.

"Sweetheart, you're so beautiful when you get angry," he says, looking straight at her with his deep, dark eyes. And Lucidity melts under his gaze, just as she did those many years ago, when it all began.

And they go home, and Rickety fucks her in the ass like he's never done before.

But we don't get to see *that* scene. All we see is the famous heart.

And the credits.

Novel of Ideas

I wrote a novel of ideas. A novel about big ideas. It was a big novel. Over 500 pages. Crammed with ideas. At least one idea on every page, sometimes more. One page even had 15 ideas. And I mean 15 discrete ideas, not variations on an idea or two. Fifteen discrete ideas. On one page. Imagine if I had 15 ideas on each page. That would be over 7,500 discrete ideas. But let's say it's more like 1,200 ideas, maybe 1,500—still a bit much, even for a novel of ideas. So I decided I'd have to edit it down. Cut the ideas down to a manageable number, manageable both for me the writer and for the reader. So I worked for months on my novel, trying to get it under control. Eight months, maybe nine, of intense work, nine or ten hours a day, about as long as it took me to write the first draft of the novel, and this is what I ended up with.

Your Novel Approach

Dear Tess (or whatever it is you call yourself these days),

It is as if everything happened so many years ago, so long ago that calendars would long since have become clocks locked in hock shops like so many cocks in shock, tenderness prickly, pricks sickly and radio irreplaceable by talkies, television and torture, as tumescent tango singers told all or nothing. Yet your recipe for stew was a novel one, and your novels unpublishable, in this or any other country. Isn't that true? Where are we?

Your recipe for stew, yes, and your novels too, but first the stew. It was not the making of the stew that intrigued me, but that hitherto unmentionable ritual, the naming of the stew, an age-old question: After whom do you name a stew? But first the making of the stew and your novel approach. Take a steak, allow time to do the work, i.e. putrefaction, maggots and the ravages of tender loving care, and when it seems appropriate to call it so, call it stew. Hence your novel approach, unpublishable until the industry comes of age. The naming of the stew and the making of the stew are of a piece. It still baffles me how those Vikings at Penguin and those penguins at Viking could turn down your novel of life in the fast lane, *No Stew on My Shoe.* Your prefabricated reminiscences of after-hours visits to shoe stores, both independent and chain, of kinky sex in stewpots, of the pros (too numerous to recount in my humble *precis*) and cons (mostly economic) of using cocaine as a genital desensitizer, seemed tailor-made for the ravenous appetites of the nouveau literate, yet no house could provide a home for your minor masterpiece. Injustice, I say.

Your face, your grace, the charm of you, not to mention the most perfect buttocks this side of Renoir, all these I fell for, but most of all it was your novel approach, and your knowledge of arcane positions unlisted even in the Vatican edition of the *Kama Sutra*. The one called "the stewpot" was my favorite, but "literary lunch" ran a close second, with "brown oxford" close behind. And you still found the time to approach your novel from a different angle each and every morning, rain or shine, like a mailman, like a milkman, and every inch a woman to boot, as you said to me, half joking, half mocking, "Quick, lick my shoes while they're still in the box."

The first time we kissed you chewed my tongue thoroughly, having read somewhere that this was the proper thing to do. I cannot say I found it wholly unpleasant—that is, the act itself was pleasurable, but the aftermath cause for regret. The things I said afterwards, and the way I said them, are unforgivable, but certainly forgettable, don't you remember?

Consorting with The Great Unknown, as you liked to call yourself, was my pleasure, my sport, my meat and potatoes, the stewpot in which I willingly swam, as you stirred up feelings in me I had forgotten I was capable of, like mild disgust, intermittent insecurity, quasi-narcissistic self-loathing, onanistic allegiances to the more humorless factions of the left wing, and last, but certainly not least, True Love, or at the very least a reasonable facsimile thereof. I'm talkin' about you and me, Toots.

Your recipe for Everlasting Happiness (or was it Happiness Everlasting?) was exquisite. Time, putrefaction, maggots, crushed tomatoes, these all figured in your equation, but it was that extra something, that secret ingredient you refuse to disclose that really made the difference. To this very day I retain vague memories of Happiness Everlasting (or was it Eternal?).

I had promised to love, honor, and obey until death, putrefaction, maggots, boredom or whim, and I have no regrets, for I worshipped you and your manuscripts. Your talent made me hard, and in a certain sense I remain that way. But this is neither the time nor place for recriminations. Could you meet me next Sunday at 6 p.m. at Sammy Wong's House of Greasy Gelatinous Chinese-American Unmentionables on West 47th Street, a longtime favorite of Broadway producers and arcade operators?

I know, I know, you had warned me that life with a genius would be difficult, but I reveled in the difficulties, difficulty held for me a certain fascination, and you held me, or a certain part of me, in the palm of your hand. To attempt to satisfy your insatiable cravings was incompatible with full-time employment, so we lived like paupers. But I was happy because I felt like a collaborator. When you dedicated your unpublished novels to my cock and your unpublished cookbooks to my tongue (or was it the other way around?), I was pleased. Words cannot express how pleased I was, as the following poem illustrates:

> When April, with its sweet and sour pork
> Avenges cruelty with a humble sneeze
> Then do the wretched henchmen of New York
> Confound their simple sophistry with cheese.

True, my art cannot compare with yours, but since you threw me out like an idea whose time has come once too often to hold even the slightest vestige of interest, my poetry has been published in the following journals:

Hog Breeder's Monthly
Progressive Grocer
The New Yorker
B.J. Review (the literary magazine of Bob Jones University, in which I published a poem titled "I Was Born Again a Thousand Times"), and in the anthology *Sixty Poets Under Seventy*, while everything you've ever written remains unpublished.

Still, I constantly think of your work. I am especially

fond of your fourth novel, *A New Life for Stu*, which you wrote in an attempt to break into the YA market.

Stu is a short-order cook at a diner called The Stewpot. When Stu is not frying eggs or slinging hash, he prepares the stew, and the first half of the novel is basically an in-depth examination of the process of stew preparation. Every morning, the owner of The Stewpot, an ancient Greek named Tantalus, supplies Stu with hundreds of pounds of steak bearing the USDA grade of unconscionable. It is Stu's job to cut up the steak into many small pieces, thereby exposing much more surface area and hastening the putrefaction process. Eventually Stu falls ill from having eaten too many scraps of the raw, rancid meat while on the job. On his deathbed, Stu repents and converts to Hinduism. He dies and comes back to Earth as a pony, and the rest of the book deals with his adventures with an emotionally disturbed boy named Mickey. I always suspected that the story was a metaphor for your working methods.

I am also fond of your seventeenth cookbook, *101 Stews on a Shoestring*, although I'm not sure whether your suggestion that the stews should literally be served on a shoestring was wholly in earnest.

What I'm trying to say is, I miss you. I am nothing without you, and that's something, isn't it? Can't we put the past behind us, the future ahead of us, and just live for today, for the moment, for the here and now? Without you there is nothing but putrefaction and maggots, but with you there is hope, which springs eternal, or is it eternally? I'm giving you ten years to reconsider. Until then, I remain

Your Humble Servant,
Stew

An Unfamiliar Method

I tried to write this using a method that was unfamiliar to me. I wrote the first sentence, only to discover it was, in actuality, the second. So I went back to square one and wondered, should that be capitalized, as if Square One were a place name? It doesn't really matter, does it? Anyway, I was unfamiliar with the method, so I had no idea whether I was doing it correctly. Still, I soldiered on. Well, I carried on, I don't know if I really soldiered on; matter of fact, what exactly does it mean to soldier on, in civilian life, that is—to carry on as if a soldier? I carried on, but I was nowhere, man. First of all, I was unfamiliar with the method, and when I'm unfamiliar with the method I get freaked out, so yeah,

> I freaked out,
> am freaking out,
> am freaking out now,

but pay no attention, I think it's a by-product of the method. Or at least that's how I calmed myself down and kept on keeping on, so to speak.

So I get here, to this point, here I am, I don't even know where I am, having kept on, carried on, soldiered on after having been stymied by an unfamiliar method. Stymied? Really it was more like an inconvenience, the inconvenience of having to cope with an unfamiliar method. If I had a familiar method at my disposal we'd be there already, but here, wherever we are, I have no idea where we are because I'm impeded by an unfamiliar method, I have no idea. Not that I'd necessarily be unimpeded by a familiar method I remember (and here I have to laugh), oh it must have been a good fifteen twenty years ago, when I was impeded by the most familiar of methods, as familiar as my right arm, one might even say, which I've been known to lift on command, on occasion. It was quite an embarrassment, I must admit. There I was, the odds-on favorite, it being well known how intimately familiar I was with the method, it not being known that, the familiar method being out of my reach, I had to resort to an unfamiliar method; flubbing it, there's no other way to say it, flubbing it—I tried blowing it, but blowing didn't sound right, not right like flubbing, so flubbing it would have to be—would have made me a laughingstock, an object of derision and opprobrium, the Village Idiot, as it were, no, that shouldn't be capitalized, village idiot, no.

Unfamiliar Tales

An Unfamiliar Face

I was staring at an unfamiliar face. I did not know this face. To me this face was unfamiliar. Unfamiliar and intriguing.

"Do I know you?" I asked her.

"Of course, darling," she said. "Of course you know me."

"But not your face," I said.

"But not my face," she affirmed.

An Unfamiliar Race

I was running in an unfamiliar race. Everything about this race was unfamiliar. Except my opponent. I knew my opponent. My opponent was familiar.

She had taken an early lead, but I finally caught up with her.

"This race is unfamiliar," I told her, through huffs and puffs.

"I thought you'd never notice," she said, and once again drew ahead of me.

Another Unfamiliar Race

On our last expedition we encountered an unfamiliar race. "This is startling," I said to my companion. "I thought for sure all the races of the world had been discovered by now, yet this one is completely unfamiliar."

"Well," she replied, "this race is obviously a well-kept secret."

An Unfamiliar Lace

I found a shoelace on the floor. It was not one of mine. As far as I could tell it was not one of hers. It was a man's lace. The kind of shoelace you'd find on a man's shoe. I picked it up. I showed it to her. I dangled it in front of her face and said, "Whose lace is this?"

"I don't know," she replied, "but I hope he gets home all right."

An Unfamiliar Case

The chief assigned me to an unfamiliar case. I was unfamiliar with the particulars of the case. When I asked her for some specifics, explaining that I couldn't solve the case unless I had some leads, she replied, "First find the case, *then* solve it."

An Unfamiliar Grace

The woman looked familiar. So I followed her. I followed her for blocks and blocks. I kept looking at her, but I still couldn't be sure.

"Excuse me, Miss," I said, "but could you tell me your name?"

She turned to me, and in an unfamiliar voice said, "Grace."

An Unfamiliar Pace

There was something different about her heartbeat. Her heart was beating at an unfamiliar pace.

What could be the cause of this unfamiliar pace? I wondered. Could it be something I said? Something I did?

I was reluctant to broach the subject, so I ruminated for a while on the beating of her heart. After some time had passed I finally decided to ask her the cause of the change, but by that time it was no longer necessary, as her heart had already returned to a more familiar beat.

An Unfamiliar Taste

I was quite familiar with her cooking, so you can imagine my surprise when I happened upon an unfamiliar taste.

"Something tastes unfamiliar," I told her.

"I tried something different this time," she said. "Do you like it?"

"I guess so," I said, "but what's different?"

"I'm not sure," she said, "but if you like it I'll make it again."

An Unfamiliar Gaze

I saw her staring out the window with an unfamiliar gaze. It was a gaze that I had never seen before. I wondered what could be responsible for her unfamiliar gaze.

"What are you staring at?" I asked her.

"It's the most amazing thing," she replied. "Come, take a look for yourself."

I joined her at the window and took a look. She was right. It was truly the most amazing thing I had ever seen.

An Unfamiliar Phase

I was going through an unfamiliar phase.

"I don't know you anymore," she told me. "You've become a stranger."

"Don't worry," I replied, "it's just a phase."

An Unfamiliar Phrase

We were having a conversation when all of a sudden I uttered an unfamiliar phrase. I became flustered, began to apologize. "I don't know where that phrase came from," I told her. "I assure you, it's an unfamiliar phrase."

"It's nothing to be ashamed of," she told me. "According to Chomsky, it's perfectly normal to utter an unfamiliar phrase every once in a while."

An Unfamiliar Maize

The last time I dined at the reservation, she served me an unfamiliar maize. "This maize is unfamiliar," I told her. "I do not know this maize."

"Oh, cut the corn," she replied.

An Unfamiliar Vase

The flowers were sitting in an unfamiliar vase. I did not know that vase. To me that vase was unfamiliar. So I questioned her. I questioned her about the vase.

"Where did you get that vase?" I asked her.

"What vase?" she asked.

"*That* vase," I said, pointing at the vase in question.

"Oh, *that* vase," she said. "I thought you gave it to me."

An Unfamiliar Ace

All right. This time I had her beaten. I was holding four kings and the ace of spades.

So I wagered everything.

And lost.

She showed me her hand. Four aces. Ace of clubs, ace of hearts, ace of diamonds, and a fourth ace. An unfamiliar ace.

An Unfamiliar Place

So there we were, the two of us, once again, in an unfamiliar place.

Riddles

White, but without wheels, it invites discussion. Clinging to a favorite line, it reveals another, identical but for one important detail. These two together are less than before yet more than another.

Some say it smells like sex after eighty. Those who have read Chomsky smile knowingly at its mention. Chomsky himself often has some with his oatmeal.

Underfed, yet fatter than a pleasant memory. A certain distortion occurs under artificial light. Thousands of out-of-work actors call it home.

Her penis stretches from here to Malaysia and back. Her incredible wealth has nothing to do with this fact. She is neither transsexual, transvestite, nor hermaphrodite.

If you scratch it, it will leave town. Its repertoire includes Donizetti, Gorgonzola, and Malaria. Ten years ago it would have been impossible.

Like a fine whine, it improves with rage. It is a thorn in the side of beef and a staple of the stenographer's diet. Its volume is 23, its mass B-minor, and its character Dickensian.

His place in history is secured by a singular act of indifference. He always wore his cap with the visor facing west. At the age of six he was already a child.

It has the texture of dandruff, the color of chastity and the aroma of half-baked ideas. The poor can easily afford it, yet it is well beyond the grasp of the wealthy. Nutritionists consider it an excellent source of iron and starch.

Bursting at the seams with inference, it dominates the landscape. To savor the full effect, one must throw caution to the wind. Underwear is wholly superfluous.

It swims in the antithesis of opposition. Its nutritional value is pegged to the dollar. No fisherman wants to catch it.

More fragrant than suicide, it quivers when gently rubbed. Like a vagrant prestidigitator's careless embrace, it is cherished by the sleep-deprived. Only when taken to task does it show its flagrant indifference.

In the morning it walks on two legs, in the afternoon on a hundred, and in the evening on four. Its body is composed of a combination of radio interference and good intentions. Its howl is worse than its overbite.

Its corrosive properties are tempered by its sunny disposition. The French name for it translates roughly as "venerable canary fodder." It is a cherished plaything of scrofulous little boys.

As a baby, he startled his parents with his vast knowledge of pre-Columbian mating rituals. As a young boy, he developed an allergy to all but the driest of water. In college, he fell from the top of his class to his death.

Neither animal, vegetable nor mineral, it nonetheless tastes like chicken. Because of its unwieldy size and shape, the Chinese abjure it. Like solitude, it is a dish best served dry.

Protected by a façade of shadows, its vulnerability only comes out at night. It can only be described using circumlocutions in vulgate Euskera. Treating it kindly, experts say, only serves to encourage it.

In the grand scheme of things, it falls somewhere between afternoon tea and genocide. While not everybody's cup of

WHISTLER'S MOTHER'S SON

tea, those who support it do so with gusto, vigilance and sweet nothings. It has nothing to do with tea.

Enhanced, but not augmented, it sleepwalks rapaciously. Winnowed to a semblance of honor, it merely desecrates the prom. That, along with a couple of erections, seals the deal.

Old by the new definition and new by the old one, it is timeless, but not ageless. Its material is of no consequence other than to provide a snapshot of a certain place at a certain time. When it's over, it's finished.

He sports Elizabethan apparel inappropriate for a man of his age. Though highly literate, he cannot see the writing on the wall. His favorite color is a pustulant off-white.

Capable of neither laughter nor tears, they nonetheless emote in their own peculiar way. A rabbi, a priest and a minister were once caught in bed with one. It takes fourteen of them to screw in a light bulb.

A sinner by trade and a laggard by avocation, he swims upstream to spawn. His penis has been featured in numerous Broadway musicals. He retains borrowing privileges at the Library of Alexandria.

Once popular pets among the lumpenproletariat, they are now relegated to the dustbin of bestiality. Their coats hang on their frames like closet Gauguins. If not neutered, they can become positively negative.

A little green in the nose, it sleeps haltingly, in tips and ends. Renegade beta-testers have been known to repurpose it for various and sundry kinds of love. It is the ultimate manifestation of agitated serenity.

A convert to Zoroastrianism at the age of 12, he is able to hold his breath for 13–15 minutes on a good day. Paparazzi tail him every time he goes to the men's room. His best-known fashion statement is a codpiece padded with foregone conclusions.

It is redacted with redacted and redacted. When flipped over it flips out. Its texture resembles the symptoms of a rare tropical disease that was stamped out ages ago.

It is horny in the morning, horny in the afternoon, and hungry in the evening. A small sect of epicene Ancient Romans worshipped it in their own way. In an obscure alphabet it spells disaster.

While technically edible, it has the flavor of rancid goat entrails topped with notes of bulimic bedbug and tin earwax. Supply and demand always remain in perfect balance, ensuring that the price is always right. Though used as a marital aid in certain preliterate societies, it more commonly functions as a reminder.

In her long and varied career she only experienced 15 nanoseconds of fame. Her fan club was started by a peripatetic cleric with an eye for small things who happened to be in the right place at the right time. Her nickname roughly translates as "The Coterminous One."

Some call it a feeling, others call it a hunch. It is especially prevalent among Manchurian house painters. There is no known cure for it.

Once found in every well-stocked cupboard, it is now considered a culinary curiosity from a more innocent time. Victorian housewives often discussed its aphrodisiac properties among themselves in hushed voices. Its English name derives from a mistranslation of the Slavonic original.

It has been likened to a cross between the dance of death and peanut butter. On the Indian Subcontinent, over a billion people have never seen, touched or even heard of it. American politicians of all stripes fear it as they fear little else.

It has the wings of a snow white dove and the feet of a clay pigeon. Neither a patsy nor a stoolie, it can mesmerize a toddler for hours on end. Kaiser Wilhelm once mistook one for a jelly roll.

The Man Who Lived in a Shoe

There once was a man who lived in a shoe. He didn't have any children. He didn't have a wife either. It was a pretty small shoe, so there was just enough room for the man. There wasn't room for any furniture, just the cushioned insole he used for a bed. He didn't have a kitchen or a bathroom because even if there were enough room it would be pretty hard to find a shoe that has plumbing.

So this guy must have been hungry and dirty all the time, right? Not at all. The man's best friends lived in the house right next door to his shoe. They were happy to let him cook in their kitchen and use their bathroom whenever he needed to. The man's friends were named Mr. and Mrs. Newhouse.

The man in the shoe's name was Moe Foote. You probably think it's funny that a guy named Mr. Foote would live in a shoe. Well, his name was precisely the reason he lived in a shoe.

When he was a kid the other kids were always saying, "Hey Foote, you belong in a shoe." At first he got annoyed any time some kid said it, because you can't help what your last name is. At least if you have a silly first name you can blame your parents, but even they had no choice about their last names.

Eventually, however, Moe began to feel differently. You might think he was a little crazy, but all of a sudden he started saying to himself, "Perhaps my name is my destiny. Maybe I was meant to live in a shoe."

As soon as he was old enough to live on his own, Moe bought the shoe and moved into it. Luckily he quickly made friends with the Newhouses. He found a job in an office that he liked a lot, and he was able to save lots of money, because it's pretty cheap to live in a shoe.

WHISTLER'S MOTHER'S SON

Then one day Moe Foote got some terrible news. His friends, Mr. and Mrs. Newhouse, told him they were moving. "We've lived in this house for ten years," Archie Newhouse told Moe. "When we moved here the house was brand new. Now it's ten years old. That's pretty old as far as I'm concerned. You can't stay in an old house if your name is Newhouse."

Moe Foote tried to make friends with his new neighbors, but they weren't interested in having a total stranger invading their kitchen and bathroom at all hours.

So you're probably thinking this story has an unhappy ending. I'll bet you think Moe became all dirty and smelly and hungry and even lost his job because of it. Well you're wrong!

Once Moe discovered he couldn't count on his new neighbors to keep up the old arrangement he left the shoe and moved into a nice new apartment.

I never said he was stupid.

No Crime

The patterns in the key sent in by the sea made the sun seem an unusual one. He'd been watching for clues, and he tried to moo for them too. The scene was eerie, it was weary of a murder. He had tried to grease the police, but they put him off. They didn't want an outside dick to stick his nose in. So, fearing a kick from the cops, and throwing a bone to his woes, he decided to go it alone. Only there was a problem: His private erection collection was occupying his attention.

He walked through the sense of the fence, past the dead beside the shed. Inside the victim was found, knife wound in his chest. On a nearby desk lay a floor plan, covered with sand and cream from an abandoned evergreen. On the map, in one corner, was a mourner, surrounded by a broken circle. The mourner held an arrow that pointed to a narrow window. He looked out, thought he heard a shout, and ran to take a closer look. The tree shook and he thought he glimpsed a familiar shape. An apparent rape in the leaves kept him probing. But no, it was an illusion, the conclusion to a futile search. There was nothing in the tree, there was no crime. The cops, ungreased, ungrimed, had set him up for their own good time. I'll get even with the cops he swore, and he swallowed the key, and the sun followed, and the earth froze, and the cops died, and the mourner in the corner cried.

A Crush on Broccoli

There once was a man who had a crush on broccoli. He didn't just like broccoli, he literally had a crush on it. He felt he could spend the rest of his life with broccoli, if broccoli would only agree to be his and his alone. So one day he asked a floret if it would marry him. He got no answer. My little floret is very shy, he told himself. I'll just give it time. All the time it needs. I'll be patient. I'll let it sit on my kitchen counter until it makes up its mind. Surely my floret will come around eventually, he thought, confident in his own charms. And the floret did eventually yield, but by that time the man no longer found it in the least bit appealing, and he threw it on the compost heap.

Bitter Garnish

The parsimonious parson parceled out parsley and ammonia as a garnish. The parishioners, perusing their plates, were assaulted by the fumes. Fuming, they gave the parson a piece of their collective mind, pummeling him to a bloody pulp for his pettiness. The chastened parson, asking the parishioners' pardon, piled their plates with parsnips and persimmons aplenty, appeasing them and earning himself a place at the table, if not yet back in their hearts.

Movies Through the Years: Forgotten Treasures from Our Archives

The Imperceptible Twitch, 1903. Overshadowed in its day by *Electrocuting an Elephant*, which was released the same year, this long-forgotten Edison effort is a true minimalist masterpiece.

William Henry Harrison, 1916. D.W. Griffith's pioneering real-time chronicle of Harrison's brief and uneventful presidency will be shown in its original, uncut thirty-day version. Look closely at Vice President Tyler—yes, it's none other than Lillian Gish in drag!

The Schvartzer Sings Kol Nidre, 1928. Early talkie about a black blues singer who turns his back on fame and fortune to become a cantor in a synagogue. Stars Blind Lemon Jefferson, with Fannie Brice as the love interest.

A Close Shave, 1936. Tod Browning's hilarious screwball comedy about two bearded ladies and an unsuspecting barber. Jean Harlow and Bela Lugosi are the ladies and Cary Grant plays the barber.

Song of the Ring, 1941. Disney's animated feature version of Wagner's masterpiece. Features Jiminy Cricket as Wotan, Mickey Mouse as Siegfried, and Dumbo as Brunhilde.

And the Army Gets the Beans, 1944. Ronald Reagan, Andy Devine and Gabby Hayes star in this wartime romp about three misfits who peddle counterfeit war bonds door to door and end up making license plates for Uncle Sam.

The Spaghetti Thief, Italy, 1949. A young boy who has lost his way wanders the back alleys of Rome one Wednesday night as his mother relentlessly calls out, "An-tony!" After two and a half hours, frustrated and hungry, he steals a box of spaghetti from the basket of a parked bicycle.

I Married a Bolshevik from Uranus, 1955. A woman wakes up one morning to discover that the slimy red creature in her bed is not the man she married. In 3-D, with Forrest Tucker and Beverly Garland.

Miracle in Westport, 1958. Cecil B. DeMille's final film, this bedroom farce with biblical overtones stars Doris Day as an unwed mother who claims immaculate conception and Rock Hudson as the repentant ad man who joins a suburban monastery. Gig Young makes a cameo appearance for no apparent reason.

Fists of Angst, Sweden, 1971. Ingmar Bergman's only martial arts film, with Bruce Lee and Max von Sydow representing good and evil.

Le Mouchoir Eternel, France, 1975. Bittersweet French comedy/drama about a young girl doomed to experience the joys and sorrows of first love over and over and over.

Back to '86, 1987. Martin Scorsese directed this tale of an unbalanced insurance salesman (Robert De Niro) who travels one year back in time and can't tell the difference.

The Bubble

Joey Gilroy set the record in the early thirties, and to this day nobody has even come close to breaking it. An amazing thing happened that day, June 24, 1933. It was the first (and, it turns out, last) annual bubble-blowing contest, sponsored by the Fleer Chewing Gum Company, at a park in Philadelphia, PA. Hundreds of contestants turned out for the event, all expert blowers, some coming from as far away as Australia. The contest was covered by all the news-reels, though no footage can be found today—all we have are word-of-mouth accounts. The way I heard it, there was no limit as to how many pieces of gum a contestant could use, and most seemed to try between four and six. Most of the contestants were pretty good, I'm told—it was not uncommon to see bubbles the size of basketballs, and many were considerably larger. But then there was Joey Gilroy, an eight-year-old ragamuffin, who used only one piece of gum, all he could afford. With his lone piece of Dubble Bubble, Joey outdid all of them. Reports differ, but one version has it that Joey began blowing his bubble at 1 p.m. and did not finish until well into the next day, by which time he had blown a bubble equal in size to the Earth itself, and the Earth promptly shriveled to nothingness while Joey's bubble attracted, like a magnet, all the Earth's surfaces, its land and seas, all its nations, its animals, its plants and people. That was back in 1933, and those who believe that version also warn that Joey is getting on in years, that his breath control just ain't what it used to be, and it's only a matter of time before everything, and everybody, blows up in Joey's face.

The Return of Amelia Earhart

When Amelia Earhart finally returned, several years into the Reagan presidency, a banquet was given in her honor. Exultant friends, senior citizens all, and admirers, many of whom had not yet been born when Amelia disappeared somewhere in the Pacific, back in 1937, showered the triumphant, if somewhat tardy, flier with gifts and kisses. An international dinner was prepared by a team of the world's finest chefs. Everybody was ecstatic—everybody, that is, except for Amelia. While her friends reveled in her good fortune, the aged aviatrix was depressed and withdrawn. She felt strange among people after all these years. And when asked for details of her great adventure, and her many seasons in limbo, she would reply, simply, "I once was lost, but now I'm found," in an uninflected monotone, wishing she had not cheated history, and yearning to return to her simple life among the shells and sponges.

The Shell

It's January 27 in Norman, Oklahoma, and Wallace Stanton, eighty-seven years old, Wally to his friends, thrice married, thrice widowed, sits in a tattered old armchair, holding a seashell to his ear, the left one, the good one, from daybreak till nightfall, just sits, shell to ear, waiting. It's January 27, and Wally listens to the shell, just as he has every January 27 for the past sixty-two years. January 27, Wally's anniversary, as is April 14 and June 11, but January 27 was the first one, Wally's first wife and first love, Amanda. January 27, the day they married and the day she died, one year later, their anniversary, a vacation in the South Pacific, January 27, the day she drowned, and the day on which, every year, without fail, without explanation, though wives two and three, Christina and Jane, certainly must have asked, Wally listens.

The Island

It started with mud but soon progressed to molten lava. That's how the island was formed. We'd heard of coughing blood, but coughing mud? This apartment is small, we hardly have room for the first island, I have no idea what we'd do with a second one. It's not his fault, I know, he's only four years old, but we can't go on like this. Something's got to be done.

We decide to sew his mouth shut. It's the only answer. But it's not easy. He's coughing and spitting mud and sand and twigs and stones, you name it. Margaret stuffs his tongue back in his mouth as I do the stitching. It takes some doing, but finally he's all sewn up. Sorry Lester, we had no choice.

It's a sickening sight. Lester's head is turning red, now purple, blowing up, two, three times its normal size. Stand back, Margaret!

Poor Lester's head explodes and out flies a flock of pigeons, but not just any pigeons, mean pigeons, nasty pigeons. There's got to be hundreds of them, maybe thousands, vicious, screeching, squawking pigeons, and they head straight for the island, Lester's island.

Well, Margaret, it looks like little Lester's dead and we're stuck with an island full of nasty pigeons.

The Man Who Knew Too Much

There once was a man who knew too much. He knew so much he couldn't even begin to tell you what he knew. He knew so much everybody called him a know-it-all. But he wasn't a know-it-all at all. He didn't know it all, just too much. This man had absolutely no desire to know it all. Already it was too much just to know too much. He couldn't keep track of all he knew. It was almost as bad as knowing nothing. Someone would ask him a question, and it could be the simplest question, and he could never come up with an answer. Not that he didn't "know" the answer, chances are pretty good he knew the answer, somewhere, in the back of his mind, but he just couldn't find it among all the knowledge that cluttered his brain so thoroughly that if you fell into conversation with him you'd likely find him to be the stupidest man you've ever met.

Mr. Beasley Pays a Visit

a farce

John and Jane Doe are at home, eating dinner, when the door-bell rings.

Jane: Doorbell, dear.

John: Yes, dear.

Jane: Well, aren't you going to answer it?

John: Yes, dear.... Why, it's Mr. Beasley, the mailman!

Jane *(shouting)*: Hello, Mr. Beasley.

John: But Mr. Beasley, why are you wearing a black suit instead of your mailman's uniform?

Mr. Beasley: Ah, Mr. Doe, this is our new uniform. Ever since the postal service was merged with the NSA for budgetary reasons, we wear black suits.

John: Well, I'm sure thankful Congress came up with that solution. I'd have hated to see you lose your job, and us lose our mail delivery.

Mr. Beasley: Yes, Mr. Doe, I'm thankful too.

John: So what brings you here so late?

Mr. Beasley: Ah, Mr. Doe, I'm afraid that's the way it's going to have to be from now on. Domestic surveillance is now our priority, and mail delivery takes a back seat.

John: Oh well, I'm glad you could make it, however late. Do you have any mail for us?

Mr. Beasley: Yes, I do.

John: Would you care to join us at the table? Perhaps have a drink?

Jane: Yes, Mr. Beasley, please do.

Mr. Beasley: Well, that's mighty friendly of you. Don't mind if I do.

(Beasley sits down at the table and takes his shoes off. His socks have holes, and several toes are sticking out.)

Mr. Beasley: These long hours are a killer. It's nice to rest my aching dogs for a few minutes.

John: P-U!

Jane: Well, Mr. Beasley, I'm sorry to hear about your long hours.

Mr. Beasley: Well, you know what they say: Neither rain, nor snow, nor slush, nor sleet, nor hail, nor freezing rain, nor thunderstorms, nor scattered showers, nor light drizzle, nor hurricanes, nor monsoons, nor dust storms, nor extremes of heat or cold can keep us from our appointed rounds.

Jane: My, that's a long list.

Mr. Beasley: Oh, that's nothing. Did you know that the Eskimos have 23 words for snow? Mookta, mookta-nu, nana-tukna, nata-nukma-nu, mata-nootka, nootma-na, nata-tooka, mook-mook, aka-natka, akta-mano, kota-kinok, nooka-mooka, mooka-nooka, poka-tooka, tooka-moka, pako-nako, nako-tooka, nooka-pako-poka, poko-noko-nana, nomo-kono, mata-kono and nooka-paka-nu.

John: That's fascinating!

Jane: But Mr. Beasley, you said there were 23 words for snow, but you only mentioned 22.

Mr. Beasley: You're very attentive, Mrs. Doe. I was just testing you. I left out mooka-nootka-pako-nana-kono-moki.

(Pause.)

Jane: Well, Mr. Beasley, can we get you something to drink?

Mr. Beasley: An egg cream would be nice.

John: I'm afraid we don't have the fixings.

Mr. Beasley: In that case, a Wild Turkey on the rocks.

John: Coming right up!

(John pours the bourbon over ice and hands the glass to Mr. Beasley, who makes slurping noises as he drinks.)

John: So, Mr. Beasley, do you have any mail for us?

Mr. Beasley: As a matter of fact I do. *(He pulls a letter out of his bag.)* Here's one from The Sooner or Later Collection Agency. *(He opens the letter and begins to read it out loud.)* Dear Mr. Doe, your account has been referred to us for collection by Throbwell Industries. As you are no doubt aware, your account with them is in serious arrears. You have ignored repeated requests to remit the amount of $45.99 owed for the Tammy Tush Love Doll with vibrating Greek features, plus postage and handling, which you ordered last October 17. You have enjoyed this product for over a year, but our client has received no payment. Throbwell Industries guarantees satisfaction, and they demand the same in return. They will stop at nothing to get it. There are no free rides on Tammy Tush. You owe, and you're going to pay. Now, as you may already know, federal law prohibits us from calling your phone in the wee hours of the morning or making blatant threats, so we can't tell you what we're going to do if you don't pay, but we can assure you, you'll pay. Sincerely, The Sooner or Later Collection Agency.

Jane: John, dear, I didn't know you had a love doll.

John: I assure you, dear, you're my only love doll. Clearly

there's been a mistake. Mr. Beasley, can I see that letter? *(Beasley hands him the letter.)* Aha!

Jane: What is it, John?

John: This letter is addressed to a different John Doe.

Jane: There's more than one?

John: There must be. This letter is addressed to John Doe, 2500 Main Street, Anytown, USA. We live at 250 Main Street.

Mr. Beasley: There is no 2500 Main Street. The highest number on Main Street is 2499, so naturally I assumed the sender had made a mistake and added an extra zero.

John: Oh, you assumed, did you? Well, then, couldn't you also have assumed they erroneously added one and actually intended the letter for 2499 Main Street?

Mr. Beasley: I suppose so.

John: Well, is there a John Doe at that address?

Mr. Beasley: There is, but it couldn't be him. That's Reverend John Doe of the Anytown Episcopal Church.

John: Well, it's either him or me, and it ain't me, so it's gotta be him.

Mr. Beasley: Could be, but if it is, I'm not at liberty to say.

(Pause.)

Jane: Any other letters?

Mr. Beasley: Oh, I've got plenty of letters. A whole bagful. Nothing else for you, though.

Jane: Oh, that's a shame. I was so in the mood for another letter.

Mr. Beasley: Tell you what, then. Since you're such a good audience, I'll read you some of my other letters.

John: Your other letters?

Mr. Beasley: Sure, everybody else's letters.

John: Is that kosher?

Mr. Beasley: Kosher, halal, that I don't know, but we all do it. *(He pulls out another letter, opens it and begins to read.)* To the occupant of Apartment 5H, 250 Main Street.

John: Hey, that's this building!

Jane: Yes, and the occupant of Apartment 5H is John Q. Public!

Mr. Beasley: Ahem. Dear occupant of Apartment 5H and frequent visitor to my apartment, 3B. I find this difficult to say, but I think the best approach is to come clean and just say it. I know we've had lots of good times together, and I'll always have fond memories of those times. I hope you'll believe me when I tell you that you really are something special, but, well, the truth is, I've met someone else, and it's time to call the whole thing off. Please promise that if we should happen to run into each other in the elevator or the laundry room you won't treat me like a pariah. Sincerely, the occupant of Apartment 3B.

John: 3B? Why, that's Nancy Drew's apartment!

Jane: That sweet little detective? Isn't she like 16 years old?

John: Actually, she turned 18 a few months ago.

Jane: Still, I can't believe she's been having an affair with John Q. Public. He's old enough to be her great-grand-father.

Mr. Beasley: *(Pulls out another letter.)* Here's another one. To the occupant of Apartment 6D, 250 Main Street. Dear occupant of Apartment 6D and frequent visitor to my apartment, 3B. I find this difficult to say, but I guess honesty is the best policy. I know we've had some good times together, and I'll always retain fond memories of those times. I hope you'll believe me when I tell you that you really are one of a kind, but, well, truth be told, I've met another man and we can't go on seeing each other. Please promise if we run into each other in the elevator or the laundry room you won't treat me like a stranger. Sincerely, the occupant of Apartment 3B.

John: Who lives in 6D?

Jane: 6D. Hmm, let me think. 6D, 6D, yes, that would be Michael J. Pollard.

John: You mean that funny looking little feller from *Bonnie and Clyde*?

Jane: Same one.

John: I had no idea he lived in this building. I always wondered what happened to him.

Jane: Well, apparently he's sleeping with Nancy Drew.

John: Not any more he isn't!

Mr. Beasley: *(Pulls out another letter.)* And for my next number... To the occupant of Apartment 2J and frequent visitor to my apartment, 3B. I find this extremely difficult to say, but I guess I just have to go ahead and say it. We've had some great times together, and you showed me many things that someone my age is rarely privy to. I will always have fond memories of our time together, not to mention those things. You're really a sweetheart, and I wouldn't do anything to hurt you, but the truth is, I've met the man of my dreams. It's like he fell from heaven, just for me. So, I'm afraid we can't go on seeing each other. But please, if we should run into each other in the laundry room or the elevator,

I hope you won't treat me like some kind of monster. Sincerely, the occupant of Apartment 3B.

Jane: Goodness. She could have saved some time if she had come up with a form letter.

John: It's pretty close already. So, who lives in 2J?

Jane: I think that's Mr. Moto.

John: The little Japanese feller with the funny voice?

Jane: Same same.

John: And he was screwing Nancy Drew? It looks like every man in this building has gotten into her apartment at one time or another.

Jane: Every man?

John: Well, dear, let me amend that. Every man but one.

(Pause.)

Mr. Beasley: So, folks, care for another?

Jane: Gee, I'm not sure.

John: I'm sure. This is getting good. Dish!

Mr. Beasley: To the occupant of Apartment 4C and frequent guest at my apartment, 3B.

John: Hold it. No need to go on. Jane, dear, who lives in 4C?

Jane: Oh, that's Lady Chatterley. She just stopped by to borrow some sugar earlier today.

John: Do you mean to tell me Nancy Drew is Lady Chatterley's lover? That would make that little detective bisexual.... Wait a minute, are you sure Nancy Drew lives in 3B?

Jane: I think so.

John: I seem to remember the Hardy Boys living in 3B.

Jane: Heavens, I think you're right. That means that one of the Hardy Boys was Lady Chatterley's lover.

John: Maybe both of them.

Jane: Or maybe one of the Hardy boys is straight and the other one is gay.

Mr. Beasley: Well, folks, you work this all out on your own. I have to get going now. I've got miles to go before I sleep.

Jane: Well, Mr. Beasley, thank you for a most entertaining visit.

John: Yes indeed, most entertaining.

Mr. Beasley: I'm glad you enjoyed the letters. And remember, the all-new combined National Security Agency and U.S. Postal Service has got you covered. Toodle-oo, folks.

John & Jane: Thank you, Mr. Beasley, and goodbye!

(Curtain.)

Within Wythynnwyth, or
What I Was Eyeing

This is where I was when I was wondering. That is, when I was wondering why. It is where I was when I was all at once worried, western man, widower, womanizer, workaholic, wet behind the ears, war orphan, wimp, waltz king and washerwoman's assistant. This is where I spent the best years of my life, the worst years of my life, my early, middle and late years. It was home, and my heart was there. I hung my hat.

My life was my life. It was what I did when I was being me. It was neither here nor there, it was within. Within Wythynnwyth, which is what I called where I was. It was a place like any other place. It was what it was, where it was. It was where I could be myself. I felt at home at home.

What I'm trying to tell you is where I was when what happened happened. It was what was when I was eyeing what I was eyeing, which was something quite unlike what it wasn't. What it was I can't say, but it wasn't Dixieland jazz, it wasn't the D.A.R., it wasn't walking pneumonia, it wasn't the flavor of the month, and it wasn't you, the object of 47% of my desires.

It was she, yes she, the other one, the object of 52% of my irrational passions. She with the mouth, the great mouth, a Radio City Music Hall with tongue and teeth. I saw my first erotic film in that mouth, a film called *Triumph of the Worker Ants*. I sat next to you, your arms a foreshadowing of this and that. Remember?

I was a child of eight with the libido of an elephant in heat. I didn't understand the stirring in my loins. Where were you when I needed you? Why didn't you explain Keynesian economics, social Darwinism, nouvelle cuisine? Why did you lick your ice cream in such a suggestive manner? I loved you, I needed you, I wanted you, just as Elvis did, in a different tense, a different order.

But everything changed when she came, repeatedly. She who, yes, I eyed shamelessly. She who smiled significantly at my erection. She of the monstrous eyes, eyes that said look at me when I'm talking to you. Look at me when you think of me. I feared her as I feared the familiar.

I was at home with myself that day, playing with myself, playing house, with myself, at home. You were there in my premonitions, your warm breath fogging my future. I was within. Eyeing from within the jurisdiction of your skin. For me, within Wythynnwyth meant with you.

And I witnessed the murder with my mouth full, full of you, or the notion of you, as you killed me in my dream. We were, I believe, inside the refrigerator. Yes, within the Frigidaire, eyeing a pornographic film, *Within Miss Winthrop*. She, the other one, the actress, she played Miss Winthrop, but you took care of the stunts. Like saying, "We Winthrop women were wonderfully wet within Wythynnwyth" ten times fast. Like making French toast without eggs. Like having sex with me when you didn't feel like it. And then you killed me. I walked up to you and I asked you to dance and then you killed me. Just like that.

You see, it was you I was eyeing, you whom I didn't know, having never seen your bare breasts, your bare ass, eyeing the unseen, and when I saw what I saw I was at once ready to leave Wythynnwyth forever, to take up residence in that part of your shoulder you use to cradle the phone while you're washing the dishes.

I was sorely in need of education, about the ways of the world, about the ways of women, about the feelings I began to feel within Wythynnwyth as I eyed the two of you, together. I had outgrown our innocent little games, my love, I was ready for bigger games, more dangerous games, guilt-ridden games, games of chance. I wanted to know what it felt like when I came inside of you. Not much, you told me.

It was cruel of you to send me off to the circus at the tender age of eight because I could perform like a grown man. And that silly name they gave me—The Young Dynamo. Can I ever forgive you?

That was the year one of the Kennedys was shot. I remember because that was the day they had me fucking the bearded lady. Her beard was like Brillo. My face was red for a week.

The entire circus had me for their pleasure. This was no Ringling Brothers, no Barnum and Bailey. Fortunately, I was able to break away, with the help of a kindly pinhead named Dr. Johnson, the only freak who never laid an appendage on me.

Back in Wythynnwyth I picked up where I left off. I planted trees in Israel, watched the yule log on Christmas Eve and sang obscure Cole Porter songs from the collection of Ben Bagley. I was determined to have a normal childhood, in spite of my glandular anachronisms.

Hey you—did you mean it when you said you loved me? I never meant it when I said I loved you. It was her I loved, always her, the other one, she of the enormous nose, the beautiful fifteen-inch nose that I dreamed about night and day. Her nose spoke of power, a power that I simultaneously feared and revered.

And so you killed me. You stabbed me in the back as I came inside of you. You killed me and you asked me what I felt.

Not much, I told you, and I was once again within Wythynnwyth, eyeing what I was eyeing, which was you stabbing me over and over and over while she, the other one, the one with the hungry eyes, watched.

Call for Submissions

For this issue, we want pieces that kick you in the gut and leave your mouth bloody. We have diverse tastes. We're especially listening for under-represented voices, Midwesterners, and writers who happen to be women. We have an affinity for second-person POV in short fiction. We get a lot of submissions about death and dying, so how about some about life and living? We want your thought fragments, ramblings, disturbing imagery, nonsensical utterances, upsetting sentences, grotesque scribblings, and unsettling desires. Our goal is to produce a book every year that both children and adults can learn from and enjoy. Don't limit yourself to ghosts, zombies, monsters, and serial killers. We are storytelling for the modern brain.

Door to Door

I heard my doorbell ring earlier this morning. I was still wearing my Dr. Dentons, as I was planning a lazy morning, though, incongruously perhaps, I was already shod in my Doc Martens, an attempt to pepper my lassitude with an air of get-up-and-go. I opened the door, and standing there was a sexy nurse, '50s-style Julie London sexy, with a stethoscope around her neck, strategically placed to add a touch of mystery to her low-cut lab coat. "I'm Dr. Dolly," she said—and I silently cursed myself for my sexist assumption that she was more RN than MD—"and I represent a line of Doc Johnson's sex aids." Well, that Doc Johnson sure gets around, I thought, first dictionaries and now sex aids. I was ready to be her Boswell.

"Well, hello Dolly," I said, waving her in, ready to examine her line, hoping she was prepared to reciprocate. She walked through the threshold, but she was gone in a flash, before I could sing "Dr. Feelgood."

"Hey, what the…," I exclaimed as I turned my head and saw her on the sofa, a pre-Castro convertible, shtupping the vacuum cleaner salesman. You see, I had let this Hoover hawker in only minutes earlier, and now the vacuum guy and the good doctor, and I mean good, were raising dust on my couch.

The nerve, I thought, as I averted my eyes from the sofa and stared aghast at the pile of dirt the vacuum guy had deposited on my carpet in order to demonstrate the prowess of his machine.

A Man Who Was Always a Man

There once was a man who never was a boy, or even a baby. He was born a full-grown man. The doctors and nurses at the hospital were flabbergasted when the man's mother gave birth. Not only was the newborn a full-grown man, he was wearing a suit and a hat. When the obstetrician slapped the man on the behind he felt something strange—it was a wallet in the back pocket of the newborn man's suit pants. The doctor pulled the wallet out of the man's pocket. Inside the wallet the doctor found a driver's license. It turned out that the man's first name was George, and his last name, of course, was the same as that of his parents. When the doctor told the man's parents about this they were very upset. "We had our hearts set on Marvin," they told the doctor.

George's parents gave him up for adoption because his name wasn't Marvin, and George had to get a new driver's license because he now had a different last name. Otherwise, they all lived happily ever after.

The Big Chat

In the morning I had noticed in the TV listings that I was scheduled to be on an interview program on my local PBS station later that day. I didn't remember agreeing to an interview, so I called the station. I got a functionary on the line and said, "Hello, my name is Peter Cherches, and I've just learned I'm scheduled to be on *The Big Chat* this evening. As I don't remember having committed to this interview, I want to check to see if there's been some mistake."

"Let me connect you with the program's producer," the functionary told me. "Can I put you on hold?"

"Sure," I said.

The hold music was that old disco song "(Push Push) In the Bush."

Push, push in the bush
Push, push in the bush
Push, push in the bush
I like to do the things you like to do, too
I like to do it, do it
I want to do the things you want to do, too
So baby, let's get to it, do it...

Then somebody picked up. "Hello, Rod Bender," the guy said.

"Are you the producer of *The Big Chat*?" I asked.

"Yes."

"Well, then, my name is Peter Cherches. I just read in the TV listings this morning that I'm scheduled to be on tonight's program, and I have no memory of ever agreeing to appear."

"Ah, Mr. Cherches, so nice to hear from you again," he said.

Again? I had never spoken to this guy before. "Again?" I asked.

"Yes, we met at the taping, of course," he replied.

"The taping?"

"Yes, when we taped the episode last Wednesday. It was a great interview. We had to cut a bit for the broadcast, of course, but I'm sure you'll be happy with the result."

Was he putting me on? I had no memory of taping an interview for *The Big Chat*, and besides, the prior Wednesday I was still in Mexico, in Merida. I didn't return until Thursday. So I couldn't possibly have been interviewed for the program.

"That's impossible," I said, "I was in Mexico last Wednesday."

"Now I know you're really Peter Cherches," he said. "That last statement has your m.o. all over it! Feigning incredulity at perfectly normal events. You're a hoot!"

"Feigning shmaining," I said. "It's the truth."

"Whatever you say," he said, laughing. "8 p.m., channel 13. I know you'll be very happy with it."

What else could I say but, "All right, then, thanks for your help."

"My pleasure, Mr. Cherches," and we both hung up.

That afternoon I took my four-mile walk around the perimeter of Prospect Park, then went home to do my vocal exercises. After that I read a bit, *Les Miserables*, the Modern Library edition, which I had only recently started, and which I realized I'd probably be slogging through for weeks. At 7:30 I made myself a sandwich, prosciutto cotto and manchego cheese with black olive tapenade on a baguette, which I washed down with a bottle of Lagunitas Little Sumpin'. At 8 I turned on the TV to channel 13. This would certainly be interesting.

On the screen was the text "Special Report." The voiceover said, "We interrupt our regularly scheduled programming for this special report. We apologize for any inconvenience." It was coverage of a mass shooting in a comedy club in another city. So far the death count stood at 17. A suspect had been apprehended. A white male, about 27 years old. Survivors were being interviewed.

That's life, I guess, I thought, and returned to *Les Miserables*.

Note on Collaborations

The following collaborative pieces are part of what I call my "abandoned prose rescue project." For these pieces, I asked a number of writers I know and respect to send short, unfinished prose work for me to make something new, complete and presentable of. A rule of the game is that there's no back and forth after the work has been submitted for my treatment (except for the occasional discussion of word choice here and there).

In some cases I completed pieces that had ended midstream, also going back to unify the tone, usually trying to retain the original writer's voice. In some cases I made a composite out of several unrelated fragments. Sometimes I mainly remixed the original writer's words into a new rhythm. In one case I made a metanarrative commentary on the original, and in another I completely rewrote a piece into a style that was not usual for either myself or my collaborator.

The result is always something neither I nor the original writer could have done on our own, and all are my tributes to writer friends whose work I admire.

Behind the Calliope
(with Robert Scotellaro)

For my birthday my wife makes me a circus. She seats me by a rainbow walker who keeps falling through the blue. In the ring, a sad clown comes out and pantomimes the sinking of the Titanic. Finding his act more than I can bear, I take a stroll about the circus and discover my wife behind the calliope, making the beast with two backs with the bearded lady.

"Stop!" I shout. "Show's over!" The bearded lady runs off, clutching her garments to her hairy chest, as my wife and I stare at each other in icy silence.

I'll be getting my wife a county fair for Christmas. With an old-time Ferris wheel and an ancient dwarf who will guess her weight.

And for me, a kissing booth, manned by an oh-so-lovely bearded lady. Ooh la la!

Hemingway's Typewriter
(with Robert Scotellaro)

Warren admires himself in the mirror.

Bare-chested, puffing a corona, sipping a daiquiri, stroking his beard, he's thinking about that other life, his past life, life as a typewriter. Yes, a typewriter, but not just any typewriter, a novelist's trusty typewriter, a war correspondent's battered typewriter, Ernest Hemingway's typewriter, a 1929 Underwood. No royal blood in *his* past, no, not even a Royal typewriter, unless you consider Papa Hemingway's Underwood royalty, which he does, as a matter of fact, proudly, yes he does.

Why, you should have seen the way those keys smashed against the ribbon, the letters punching black bruises onto the page, words running across the paper with the force of inevitability, like the bulls at Pamplona. You should have seen it.

Ask not for whom the carriage returns, Warren admonishes his reflection.

Ding!

Days Lost To History
with No Eyewitness
(with Don Skiles)

Small moments. Places once lived, streets the once-familiar routine of someone else's days. Would it be an epic night, then? A Hank Williams June night in a high school gym in some small Arkansas town circa 1952? There was a motorcycle—a Ducati—parked in a thick scattering of fallen leaves, reds, especially, every hue from a deep, rich wine crimson to a soft, fading pink. It was a time for one of those small moments, when a woman walks out of a piazza on a warm, humid summer night. Most people are traveling endless highways looking for somebody they left behind. A look, a glance in the street, from someone you don't know, never did, and never will, hanging like a guitar chord in the cold night air. A song, late at night. Never come back; never return. Cold, Cold Heart.

Mercy, Mercy, Mercy
(with Don Skiles)

I had recently bought a small car, and one summer evening, a Friday, I remember, I was to drive up to my friend
Cole's cabin in the mountains, not so far from where I was
living at the time. Thirty miles, forty at most. But a sudden
summer thunderstorm came through just as I was about to
leave, with great flashes of lightning and heavy, booming
thunder. Gusts of rain buffeted the house, sounding more
like sand than water.

When it hadn't let up for an hour, I called Cole and told
him I wasn't coming. I had no sooner hung up the phone
than the rain, and the wind, stopped abruptly. I walked
around the house throwing open all the windows. I still
remember the freshness.

Nearly forty years my senior, Cole was a friend and a
mentor. When I was new at the university he had sort of
adopted me. He had just retired, after the spring semester.
He was now "emeritus."

As it turned out, I was never to see Cole again. He died
about six months later, several days after his seventieth
birthday. I had spoken with him on his birthday. "My biblical allotment," he had said with a laugh. "Three score and
ten." He knew he was ill, it turned out, but he didn't let on.
He was discovered by some neighbors out for a walk, alert-
ed by the incessant barking and whimpering of his dog.

The day I got the news, from his estranged wife, of all
people, it was snowing. I was watching the flurries through
my window and listening to the radio when the phone rang.
AM radio. There was only AM those days, really. Cannon-
ball Adderley's "Mercy, Mercy, Mercy" was playing. It had
made the Top 40. Very rare for a jazz recording.

A Red Flag and a Horn
(with Don Skiles)

The girl stands in the doorway to the kitchen, in the old house, the old home, the old town. At the table, the man drinks tea, strong, dark tea, no milk. The woman, his wife, her mother, is standing, standing tall, five-foot-eleven, very tall for a woman in these times, in 1906.

Pennsylvania, an ocean away from Donegal, and then some. They still remember Donegal. The man and the woman, that is. The girl was born here, in central Pennsylvania.

Is it raining yet, or is the man only thinking of rain, of the rain to come and thinking of the ride ahead and the mud, remembering the way it rained when it rained in Donegal?

The girl, six years old, has a serious look on her face, or perhaps a worried one. It's moving day.

A house painter, the man has decided to move the family two hundred miles away, to a small town in western Pennsylvania, not far from Pittsburgh. The Steel City is booming. "Someone'll have to paint all those houses they're building," he has told his wife and daughter.

The wagon is loaded, the horse hitched. The little girl sits in the front with her father, all the way to their new home, watching the rain fall steadily on the back of the horse ahead of them.

As they pull into the new town, their new home, the girl sees a curious and delightful thing. A man is waving a red flag and tooting a horn as a motorcar trails behind him. It's a new town ordinance, the family learns. The signalman must precede any motorcar through the town's streets, for the protection of the citizenry, and of dumb animals.

The woman dies not too long after the move, only

months. Dying young is not yet a strange thing. The man too dies a few years later, on a job, falling from a ladder, impaled on the spikes of a high, decorative iron fence. The little girl goes to live with an aunt and uncle, in Pittsburgh, in the city.

An old woman, the little girl, who has witnessed a century, still remembers the red flag and the horn, eighty years later, in 1986, in Pennsylvania, in another small town not far from Pittsburgh.

Panes of Glass
(with Melody Sumner Carnahan)

I lean against the brick side of the house in the middle of the night in the pouring rain. Earlier, the wind nearly tore the house apart. My room is the upstairs porch, my choice. Moonlight pours onto my blankets at night. And rain, when it rains. My feet are bare. I have no coat, but I never feel cold. All night long the shutters of the house have been crashing against the walls. I feel the roughness of the brick where my shoulder presses against it. And the wetness. There are over a hundred panes of glass in the windows.

Let me just say this: He didn't love me, and he knew it. I knew it too. I didn't love him. He knew it, but I didn't. Then there was his anger, rising thick and sour for no good reason, alternating with his silences.

We could have been friends, just friends, I suppose, except I guess I didn't really even like him either. Not the way he was then, self-centered and distant. And I, I confess, was vain and foolish, laughing or crying all the time, sometimes both.

The lamplight on the pavement fractures and scatters with every raindrop. There are no sounds except for the monotony of the rain.

I've heard it said that our greatest passion is laziness. It takes much more energy to love than it does to hate, and it takes a lot of energy to mature. People give up too easily, just as they fall in love too easily, never realizing that love's infancy must be nurtured. Many never get out of infancy. Most? Observing my own thoughts I'm forced to recognize the inevitable truth that envy and resentment make up most of what we call adulthood.

The apple tree has just started to blossom. Soon there will be crickets in the grass. I fear it's an illusion, but summer does seem imminent.

He often used to sit behind a massive oak desk that faced a window that looked out onto a central square with a large buckthorn tree in full flower, in silent contemplation, inscrutable. He looked thinner, the last time I saw him. Thinner, browner, happier. Not happy to see me, I'm certain, just happy.

My eyes become drawn to the oscillating movement of an open umbrella, overturned and gathering rain just beyond my reach. He throws it to me when he finally finds me, smiling.

Eggs
(with Marina DeBellagente LaPalma)

It happened so long ago and it replays, like a film, in her head, as she cracks eggs in the morning, into a bowl, and she remembers to look away, as she always does, before she beats the eggs, to scramble.

Was it minutes or only seconds that she stared into the toilet, at it? A cliché, yes, but it seemed like hours, though it was probably only a minute or two, in her numbness. She could see it again, clearly, in her mind's eye—another cliché that, "mind's eye"—thirty years later, just as she could see his face as it was thirty years ago.

She had enjoyed the pregnancy, in its early months, before it had happened, in their house in Berkeley, when she was twenty-five. But it happened. The bleeding and the cramping had begun late one night, continued into the morning, and then it was there, in the toilet bowl, for her to see, something outside her.

William was in the kitchen, making breakfast. She called to him, to come to the bathroom. "Is it really necessary?" He yelled back. "Can't it wait?"

Was it just that he was engaged in what he was doing, or had he sensed the meaning of her call? Was he being William when he shouldn't have been, the William who avoided all complexity, all confrontation, all unpleasantness? She sensed the latter and, cliché though it may be, she was sure she felt a string snap in her heart at that very moment, and from there the marriage began to unravel, though it really had begun sometime before, though it took another year for her to leave him.

She sees his face as it was thirty years ago, in her mind's eye, and she pushes the bowl aside.

Leaving the Farm
(with Norman Conquest)

The Farmer's Daughter lies in bed, dreaming of city and sin. I'm sick and tired of this Farmer's Daughter shit, she tells herself. I'm just the butt end of a flood of crappy jokes, she thinks. She dreams of running away, to a place where she can be lost in the crowd, be herself, no longer the "Farmer's Daughter" of laughter and derision.

The following morning, weary from a night of insomniac nocturnal daydreaming, she decides to take the bull by the horns and make her getaway. She rushes off to the one-lane dirt road, the town's main thoroughfare, with nothing but a small travel bag and the clothes on her back, and flags down the bus.

She sits in the back, far from the three strange men in suits, each seated alone, with fluorescent skin and foam oozing from the corners of their mouths, the only other passengers. From time to time they turn around to stare at her. One of the men, a traveling salesman, brushes and encyclopedias, a one-two punch, chats with the driver, whose eyes are glued to the rearview mirror. The Farmer's Daughter can hear snippets of the conversation. They are talking about fishing, and the salesman must be quite a good fisherman since the driver keeps saying things like, "Wow! That's something! Really?" After a while the salesman runs out of fish tales, turns to sit sideways—an unnatural position—and leers at the Farmer's Daughter. She squirms, glances down at her lap, then begins rummaging through her bag, searching for nothing, just avoiding his ogle. She looks up, catches his eye briefly, and thinks: This man looks very familiar. She averts her eyes again, as she knows if she acknowledges him he'll strike up a conversation, and conversation inevitably leads to calamity. She closes her eyes, leans back in her seat and pretends to nap. She imagines the view outside her window, the endless string of farms, a cinematic blur to her mind's eye.

When the bus reaches Los Angeles she steps into the station's waiting room. It's hot and musty. The ceiling fans are out of service, and it's the dead of summer. The benches are occupied by elderly men and women, Mexicans, the Farmer's Daughter thinks. They're seated upright as if at a church service, some wearing their Sunday best, tattered yet dignified. A few hold swizzle stick-sized American flags and wear expectant expressions, but most look as though they've lost their faith. She wonders if they are coming or going.

The Farmer's Daughter leans against a wall. She opens her travel bag to fish out her compact and out jumps an iguana. How this iguana got in her bag she does not know, but it's a particularly aggressive reptile, and it jumps on the Farmer's Daughter, taking her unawares and knocking her to the floor as it begins to rip off her clothes. She screams, but nobody comes over to her aid. The Farmer's Daughter's dress is in tatters, skin exposed, as the iguana runs roughshod over her body, scratching and biting until she's a bloody mess.

Lying on the floor, wounded, bleeding, exhausted, defeated, she hears an announcement: The bus to San Diego has arrived. The elderly Mexicans rise from their benches and proceed, single-file, expressionless, to the exit.

The Farmer's Daughter looks up and sees a flashing neon sign she had not noticed before.

"Today is the first day of the rest of your life."

Three Chinese Guys
(with Richard Grayson)

As far as I was aware, there were only three Chinese guys in the high school I transferred to in my junior year. What struck me after a few months was that none of them ever talked to the others. It was a big school; why should I have been surprised?

Su Tom was the one I had lunch with every day at the losers' table. He was fat, with really bad acne, and the most pathetic thing about him was that every day he wore what looked like the same white short-sleeved dress shirt. Maybe they were different ones, but Su Tom's father ran a Chinese laundry, so I suppose he could have washed the same shirt every day. Su Tom and I were in some of the same classes, and once a substitute social studies teacher called him Tom. Su Tom corrected her.

Howie, on the other hand, was slim and a great dresser. I was in his gym class at 7:50 in the morning, and I tried to make sure he wouldn't notice me staring at him furtively in the locker room. About ten years after we graduated, I saw him on a subway platform, and he looked as if he was on his way to an important appointment.

Henry was in my advanced drama class senior year. He was tall and chunky and laughed a lot. He played roles written for white actors except for the time he and Judy Nussbaum did a scene from *A Majority of One*, with her playing an old Jewish lady and Henry playing a Japanese businessman.

I really knew nothing much else about any of those three, I'm afraid to say.

What was I to them?

Did any of them wonder why I didn't seem to know all of the couple of hundred other Jewish boys at the school? Did they even know I was Jewish, or was I just plain-vanilla white? Was I one of those names their immigrant parents, or even second-generation, called white people, *lo fan*?

Did any of them think of me at all? I suppose Su Tom did, since we spent a lot of time together.

I like to think, all these decades later, that Howie did, but I'm sure he didn't.

Portrait of a Tobacconist
(with Eckhard Gerdes)

Friendly Tobacco. That's the name of his shop. Friendly Tobacco. Emil Friendly is a tobacconist. Your friendly neighborhood tobacconist.

A pusher, right? That's what you're thinking, no doubt, a drug pusher. A veritable nicotine candy man, as it were. Emil Friendly does sell candy too, and breath mints, while we're on the subject, but tobacco is his stock in trade.

Calling the tobacconist, the main character of this feuilleton, Friendly—that's a joke, right?

No, friends, it's no joke. Emil Friendly is an honorable man plying a venerable trade, respected since women were women and cigars were smokes. There was a time when a tobacconist had to know the difference between Latakia and Perique, Virginia and Burley, Yenidje and toasted Cavenish. How many of you, dear readers, can tell the difference between Yenidje and toasted Cavenish? Emil Friendly can. He can also spot a Peterson at twenty paces. The tobacconist's eye, the tobacconist's nose.

Tobacconist, a quaint yet stately word, so much more elegant than "smoke shop proprietor," don't you think?

Feuilleton? Can you offer me a better term?

Emil Friendly, though always chatty and cordial with his patrons, is something of a loner when not at the shop. So, actually, though his customers do consider Emil friendly, he's really something of a...well, "misanthrope" isn't exactly the word, he doesn't dislike humanity per se, he just lacks more than a passing interest in his fellow man. We need another term, one with the flavor of "agnostic."

Look over there, to the left. Do you see that house? A two-story yellow brick number in the North Shore suburbs of Chicago. There's a nice yard in front, and an even nicer yard in back (you'll have to trust me on this one). The front lawn (yes, I know I said yard) is decorated with rows of perennial flowers accented by new patterns of annuals every year. This year the last frost happened early, so the flowers are particularly stunning. Of course, the ajugas are beginning to overtake the jack-in-the-pulpits, and the squirrels keep decapitating the sunflowers, but those are the tortures suffered by many gardeners. Emil Friendly often considers poisoning the squirrels, but he can never bring himself to do so.

Emil had once traveled all the way to Turkey to meet the great Meerschaum pipe artist Ismet Bekler—the Paganini of pipe carving—so dedicated is he to his trade and its traditions. *Some may think me a pariah, but I belong, after all, to an ancient and noble profession*, Emil assures himself. Still, people are going to think the worst of him, so he buries himself in his gardening to forget his worldly woes.

In his affluent, lily-white suburban community, Emil Friendly is the sole Communist. Even namby-pamby Democrats are harder to find than a needle in the haystack of this overwhelmingly Republican enclave. At "community outreach" meetings, he continually irritates his neighbors by suggesting that the inhabitants of this town, village, hamlet, call it what you will, pool their resources in order to benefit the community as a whole.

Now, Emil doesn't consider himself a Communist, a "commie," even if his neighbors do. He claims to be an "independent." Of course, that really means next to nothing, as "independent" is a catch-all that has included, in a brief span of time, virulent racists like George Wallace, wacky billionaires like Ross Perot, moderate Republicans like John Anderson, and stern consumer advocates like Ralph Nader.

Emil Friendly is an independent tobacconist whose greatest passion is gardening.

An independent and honorable tobacconist. Emil would never sell tobacco products to anyone underage, I can assure you. Why, he'd card anyone who looked a day under 30. And what's more, he wouldn't even sell to anyone who coughed when asking for cigarettes.

"Excuse me <cough>, <cough> <cough>, a pack of Pell Mell please."

"Pall Mall? No, buddy," Emil would say, "I can't sell to you. You've had enough. Now go home and sleep it off."

Emil Friendly may not care much *for* people, but he cares *about* them, as he cares about tobacco and his garden. Gardening he very much cares for.

One Sunday afternoon, a roving philosopher, white of hair, white of beard, turns up as Emil is tending his peonies and nasturtia. "Neighbor," the philosopher announces, "there is a concatenation of events in this best of all possible worlds."

"Whatever," Emil replies. "Just let me tend my garden."

Art School Confidential
(with Bradley Lastname)

I've known Bradley Lastname since 1985. I first met him when I was in Chicago to do a performance, "Love Me Like a Bitter Pill." Lastname, as you've probably guessed, is not Bradley's real last name. A writer and visual artist, Bradley has long been a legend in the neo-dada and mail art worlds. I once did a profile of Bradley, where I wrote, "He writes like Bozo the Clown on nitrous oxide channeling the likes of Tristan Tzara, Luis Buñuel, Steven Wright, and a mischievous eight-year-old with ADD."

I invited Bradley to send me an unfinished piece for my collaborations project. I communicate with Bradley by email and I always get a response by snail mail. He sent me a piece called "Art School Confidential: A Story I Never Knew How to Finish."

But was it a story or an outline of a story? I suppose it's a story *in essence*, but the prose reads more like a description of a story. Of course, Bradley being a conceptualist, this made perfect sense.

The three sheets he sent included illustrations on two of them, to go with the story, drawings of a parakeet on a perch progressing, or rather regressing, from a fully formed bird to a simple schematic, two intersecting ovals.

Bradley's story, or synopsis, began, "The professor of art is a *failed painter* and *terminal alkie* who usually comes to class *drunk* & verbally abusive..."

To give a synopsis of Bradley's story, or a synopsis of his synopsis, the lesson this particular day is on "HOW TO DRAW A VENN DIAGRAM." Here's where the birds come in. The professor "starts by drawing a perfect parakeet, and gradually deconstructs it until he produces the Venn diagram in panel #6," i.e., the two intersecting ovals.

A student asks the professor why he doesn't just draw a Venn diagram without the preceding five panels, and the professor "lets loose with a *torrent of obscenity* that would even make Lenny Bruce blush." And that, pretty much, is the whole story, minus the ending.

Bradley writes, "I came up with 2 possible endings, but wasn't *really satisfied* with either one."

The first ending: The student, who has been told to go fuck himself by the professor, lights a cigarette lighter in front of the professor's face, causing the professor's high-octane breath to catch fire, killing him in the conflagration.

"In the *second* ending," Bradley writes, "the parakeet in the first panel springs to life and flies off the easel and pecks the professor's eyes out."

So now it's my job to finish the story. Immolation or "out of the inkwell" retribution? For me it's a no-brainer. I choose door number two. The first ending I find gratuitously violent. Sure the professor is a prick, but does he really deserve to die such a violent death? Plus, though Bradley may not have thought it out this far, surely the student would have to pay the consequences of his actions. I'm sure Bradley wouldn't want to condemn the poor student, who acted impulsively, to life in prison.

The second ending is highly preferable in several ways. It better integrates the drawings into the story, first of all. And eye-plucking has a long and honorable literary pedigree, *Matthew 5:29* and Oedipus, for instance. And he is an art professor, after all, so this is poetic justice. "If thine eye offend thee, pluck it out: it is better for thee to enter into the kingdom of God with one eye, than having two eyes to be cast into hell fire."

Wait a minute, there's the same dilemma: eye plucking vs. fire. Now I'm wondering, was this a puzzle Bradley wanted me to figure out?

Cold, a Dick, and a Maid
(with Joel Rose)

When policy abdicates morality, our age suffers, and an ordinary demonstration of a victim's immobility has little significance. Television structures its incompleteness upon our own well-formed images, causing a singular and profound anxiety. In an epiphany of official procedure, the police effect a posture that reduces immortality to a single drop of water.

Tonight. Two teenage boys loitering on the corner, laughing and joking together, waiting for customers so they can steer them the proper direction. Just like the job Cold first had, when he fourteen and ol' Cadillac Earl take him in just like a dad.

The angel of death, a hard-boiled dick, has come to interrogate the maid. Angel-dick thinks out loud: Considering the great distance a soul must travel to find its haven, I can only hope that motion sickness dies with the body.

Cold run his game from two small rundown brick houses. The houses built as two-families in the twenties, but sometime over the years each had been broken down into six small, cramped apartments. At number 52 and number 54, Cold have his agent rent two dark three-room cribs, a bedroom, a small workable kitchen and a living room in each.

For the most part the occupied apartments in the two buildings were messy and grimy and roach-infested, but Cold left strict orders not in his spots, and his people cleaned them up nice and keep them spic-and-span or face the consequences. Sometimes even a maid, if they keep watch.

Out the first apartment Cold run the dope. From the other the coin. The white powder and the cash money were never in the same place at the same time, insurance against bust or rip-off. Cold never enter these apartments. He never touch the dope, and he never touch the paper. Not until Reg G hand-deliver the jack to his penthouse after going through an intricate series of blind couriers and deceptions. In this way, if the authorities ever pick him up, they would have a hard time trailing the commodity back to him—a lesson he had learned well from Cadillac Earl Dockery (RIP), the now-dead street baron Cold had first gone to work for when he was a youngster.

The maid chides the dick, "Act in the house of a stranger as you would in the house of the lord."

The rock and white powder itself actually sell out of a hairdresser down the street, sitting between the Smiling Faces Christian Excellent Second-Hand Clothing Center and the Brothers' Community Hardware Store. The plate glass window of the hairdresser have a handwritten sign urging the people of the neighborhood to "SUPPORT ALL BLACK BUSINESS," the wisdom quote signed with the name of the great M.L. KING.

"There is no God," the suave and handsome dick says. "Ours is the age of Don Juan. It is a difficult star I follow. A Don Juan fishes for admiration, but no job is fishier than mine. What will come of it all?"

Cold palm the Bentley walnut steering wheel and swing the big car around, glancing in the rearview one last time at Big and Li'l getting in Big's midnight-blue Lexus, preparing to drive away their own selves, set out on their appointed mission of extermination.

Cold head back into his old neighborhood, into his enterprise. He stop for a red light, checking his empire, following all the traffic rules—don't want to rouse the man.

"Your job weighs heavy on your heart and soul, I can see," the maid says.

"Man's capacity for calculation has its price," the dick replies. "I used to be an exterminator, you know. I did away with insects

and parasites."

"I can see it in your face, sir," she says.

Used to be a dozen steerers out here on a given night, but business kinda quiet. Business been kinda quiet for many moons. Cold used to mint money out here. Control six blocks, pull in about 125 grand a week. But those Nino Brown Nicky Barnes new jack days be over.

The dick, emboldened, says, "To tango with an official avatar can be quite edifying."

"What are saying, sir?" the maid asks.

"Treat me no differently than you would a momentary twitch, or a stranger with a heightened interest in water. That's all I am, a stranger. Capeesh? Understand?"

"A stranger. I understand."

A stranger. Cold understand.

Found Photo
(with Holly Anderson)

When you live with something long enough I guess you get used to the odor and then it's no odor at all, it's part of the room, maybe it's just a dead mouse behind the wall and there's nothing to be done unless you want to take a hammer to the wall one hot, gray afternoon when it feels like ants are crawling up and down your legs, getting right into your underpants.

So here we are, all dressed up and left all alone in the shaking woods. Why did they leave us out here like this, all alone? Drive away in that brand new automobile we helped them to buy? Sure, Pop's lost a bit of his left leg, the diabetes chewed his foot right up to the shinbone, but that's no reason to throw us out here without so much as a drink of water. A smell, sure, but not a stink. And weren't they the ones always pushing sugary things at him anyway? He never was one to say no.

When you live with something long enough it's really no odor at all.

We knew it had to come off when even the dogs wouldn't go near him.

Thinking helps to pass the time.

He never did talk much, and it's especially hard to be sitting here on a bench in the absolute dead center of nowhere with a one and a half-legged man who won't say a word. Thank the Lord they didn't drive off with the crutches.

When you live with something long enough I guess you get used to it.

So here we are, left alone in the woods by our own children, and not a soul to help us, and not a drop to drink. My mouth must look like a flattened mattress by now. Or an old and faded photograph.

It's all part of life, I guess. You bring them into this world, you do your best to make a life for them, and then they have to up and leave you one day, go off on their own. I just never thought it would be like this! It's like there's a dead mouse behind the wall and there's nothing to be done unless you want to take a hammer to the wall one hot, gray afternoon when it feels like ants are crawling up and down your legs, getting right into your underpants, out in the woods, all alone, thinking to pass the time, sitting on a bench with a one and a half-legged man who won't say a word.

An old and faded photograph has an odor, but not a stench.

My Crisis

I wasn't feeling myself this morning, so I called 911.

The operator said, "911, what's the address of the emergency?"

I wasn't sure how to answer that. "I don't know," I said, "I guess everywhere."

"Everywhere?" the operator asked.

"Well, everywhere I go," I replied.

"What's the problem?" the operator asked.

"I'm not feeling myself today. I mean, I don't feel connected to myself," I said. "That is, I know who I'm supposed to be, I know my name, my past, my history, my friends and loved ones, but I don't feel like that person."

"Oh," she replied, "you're having an identity crisis."

"I guess you could call it that," I said.

"What's your name?" she asked.

"I don't know how to answer that," I said. "I mean, I know my name's Peter Cherches, but I don't feel like Peter Cherches. I can't even imagine what it would be like to feel like Peter Cherches."

"Who do you feel like?" she asked.

Who did I feel like? That was an interesting question. Who did I feel like? I certainly didn't feel like the person I was supposed to be, Peter Cherches. That is, I didn't feel like the memories were mine. If anything, I felt like someone who didn't know who he felt like.

"I'd like to find out who I feel like," I told the operator.

"Well, Mr. Cherches," she said, and it felt so weird being referred to as Mr. Cherches. "Well, Mr. Cherches, I think the best thing I can do for you is connect you with the identity crisis hotline."

There's an identity crisis hotline? Who knew?

"Would that be all right with you?" she asked.

"Yes," I said, "I suppose that would be OK."

"You just hold on a minute, all right?"

"All right."

I waited for my call to transfer. Then I heard the operator's voice again. "Hello, I'm an operator from 911 in Brooklyn, New York. I have a caller I'd like to refer to you. Would that be all right?"

"Yes," the hotline guy replied, "that will be all right."

"All right, Mr. Cherches," the 911 operator said, "is there anything else I can do for you before I leave this call?"

"No," I said. "Thank you for your help." I heard a change in the aural ambience, signaling that the 911 operator had left the conversation.

"Mr. Cherches?" the identity crisis counselor said. "Thank you for reaching out. My name is Rick. How can I help you?"

I told Rick about my problem, about how I wasn't feeling myself. He was very patient and caring. He let me speak and he would only break in to ask pointed questions when I seemed to be rambling, but even then he gave me some leeway. I don't know how long the call lasted, at least a half hour. I told him all about the life of Peter Cherches and how I didn't feel connected to it any more. He was very understanding, in no way judgmental. The kind of person I would like to be. "Maybe it's just a phase you're going through," he said. "Maybe if you just give yourself some time things will straighten themselves out."

"Maybe," I replied.

"Do you think you'll be OK on your own now? We'll always be here for you if you need us."

"Yeah," I said, "I'll be OK. Thanks for your help." And I hung up.

Maybe one day this nightmare will come to an end. Maybe one day I'll feel like Peter Cherches again. But for the time being, can you please call me Rick?

Now how can I help you?

Backwards Man

There once was a man who was backwards. Everything about him was backwards. His face was on the back of his head, and the back of his head was where his face should be. His chest was on his back and his back was where his chest should be. His feet pointed backwards, but that was the same direction his face faced. So even though he walked backwards, it looked like he was walking forwards, because the rest of what should have been the front of his body faced backwards too. In fact, since every last detail about this man's body was backwards, he never had any idea he was backwards at all, because everything looked and felt perfectly normal. And nobody else knew he was backwards either. So there's really no story after all, is there?

An Eternal Washing

One hand washes the other, an eternal washing as the one hand assumes the dirt of the other and the other, in turn, assumes the dirt of the one, ad infinitum, never the two hands clean at once, yet always meeting a need born of its own meeting.

Three Idioms

He wears his heart on his sleeve and his lungs on the legs of his trousers. His kidneys he keeps in his two back pockets. His liver dangles from a watch fob. He wears his intestines around his neck, and his brain sits atop his fedora. Were he ever to undress he would die.

His life was an open book, opening to a different page every time, but not just a different page, a different page from a different book, each and every time. Indeed, his life was a bookcase full of open books, with all the open pages facing out and all the spines hidden from view, so nobody ever knew which open book his life happened to be at any given moment. As he got older the open books proliferated, naturally, and when he died there were so many open books that he had to be entombed in the local library.

She loves him, warts and all. Not that he has many warts. There's the plantar wart on the ball of his right foot, and there are those two ugly little warts on the palm of his left hand, but that's about it. Three warts. Three measly warts. She loves him three measly warts and all. Big deal.

He Wouldn't Take No for an Answer

There once was a man who wouldn't take no for an answer. Whenever anybody responded "no" to a request, an inquiry, a plea, he'd respond, "I'm sorry, but I refuse to take no for an answer."

This man, who lived in New York, decided to move to Philadelphia. He boarded a train with all his things and asked the conductor, "Is this the train to Philadelphia?"

"No," said the conductor.

"I'm sorry," the man replied, "but I refuse to take no for an answer," and he took a seat.

The man now lives in Boise, Idaho.

At the Terminal

"Leave the driving to me," said the sadist to the masochist in the waiting room of the Greyhound terminal in Dynel Falls, PA. It was snowing outside, a blizzard, actually, an anomaly, to say the least, in August, in Dynel Falls, or anywhere in Pennsylvania, or anywhere in the U.S. of A., for that matter, except perhaps Alaska, maybe. Perhaps that's what brought Spike and Doug together—the weather, and just the fact of the two of them being there and then and simpatico to boot. So they found a place not too far away, a stone's throw, really, a perfect place to hurt and to be hurt, an abandoned gazebo overlooking the interstate.

And there the sadist demanded reverence.

And there the sadist demanded reverence.

And there the sadist demanded reverence.

And there, in the gazebo, in the freezing cold, in August, in Dynel Falls, Pennsylvania, there the masochist paid court, in ecstasy, a child again, forced to eat spinach, and hating it, and eating it, and loving it.

Reverence

A reverence most irreverent reveals an unraveling of time-traveling, alone or with a tour group consisting mostly of bored Midwesterners, a few doubting, but most still followers of a beleaguered television evangelist named T. Minus, in deep ado about something with the FCC. You see, it was the presence of partial dorsal nudity on the T. Minus Arctic Circle Crusade broadcast that led to the present hot water and the concomitant emergency fundraising bus ride to nowhere that brought our group of partially hydrogenated, non-nutritive artificial pilgrims together, bonded by no more than a eulogy and a prayer. Never before had so few paid so much for so little, and they would little note nor long remember the experience, except, perhaps, for the inevitable nocturnal emission or, pardon my French, *déjà vu*. And so they go in search of the search for the road to salvation, for nothing more or less will do except, perhaps, for the unanswered question that will open the can of worms that will, in turn, open the closed door of faith and give the faithless something to crow about.

But onward.

To your left, if you look closely, is a replica in miniature of the T. Minus Tabernacle of Greed, small enough to fit in the palm of your hand yet durable enough to last an eternity. And there's only a handful left, if you get my drift.

Something Wrong

"I think there's something wrong with her," she said to him, referring to a woman they knew in common.

"There's something wrong with all of us," he replied, referring to all of us.

The Roaring Husband

"My husband roars during sex," the first woman said to the other woman. "Does your husband roar?"

"No."

"What kind of noises does he make, then?"

"Noises? He doesn't make any noises. He's pretty much silent. Except when it's over. Then he says, 'That was nice,'" said the other.

"Oh. My husband roars," said the first, again.

"What does your husband say after it's over?" asked the other.

"'That was nice.'"

A Man Who Couldn't Decide

There once was a man who was unable to make a decision. Eggs or cereal for breakfast posed such a dilemma that he usually went without breakfast. He wanted to take a vacation, but he couldn't decide between Rome and Bangkok, so he stayed home, where he couldn't decide what to do with his time. He could never decide which shoes to wear, so he went barefoot all the time, which was a shame, because he owned twenty pairs of perfectly good shoes. He had so much trouble deciding what to watch on TV that he bought a broken set that only picked up one channel, the one where a nun sat in a chair and talked all day. Most days he couldn't decide whether to take a bath or a shower, so he was dirty and smelly most of the time.

On one of those rare days when he was clean, he met a woman and fell in love. They dated for some months. She was the perfect mate, because she made all the decisions. She decided what movie to see and what restaurant to go to. She even ordered for him at the restaurant. Then, one day, she asked him if he'd marry her, because she knew he'd never be able to make the decision to ask her. He was ecstatic that she had asked him, but he couldn't decide whether to accept. "I just don't know," he told her, day after day.

"Well, I know," she finally said. "You'll marry me."

"All right," he said, going along with her decision.

On their wedding day, the justice of the peace asked the man, "Do you take this woman to be your lawful wedded wife?"

The man just stood there, frozen. He couldn't decide. "You tell me what to do," he said to his fiancée.

"Not this time," she replied. "I've decided that this is just too important. You're going to have to decide for yourself, otherwise I'll never know how you really feel."

So the man flipped a coin.

No Return Address

About a week ago I received a large package in the mail with no return address. I opened the box and found the following: 32 eustachian tubes, 173 geraniums, three flimsy excuses, one chastity belt (extra-large), one small vial of saffron, 147 salty tears, 75 trombones, the national anthems of five former Warsaw Pact nations, four instances of righteous indignation, two pairs of white clam diggers, 133 sugarless hard candies, two cases of unrequited love, 77 lipstick-stained cigarette butts, eight sinus headaches, one old-style bottle of seltzer, one quart of milk, and a jar of chocolate syrup, Fox's U-Bet.

I removed the last three items, made myself an egg cream, and put the box out on the stoop of my building.

Then, only minutes later, I realized I really should have kept the saffron too, so I went out to my stoop, but, alas, the saffron was already gone.

Apple Blossom Time

I was spearheading a steering committee when I could no longer hold my breath. Much to my embarrassment, I exhaled. The shocked subliminal committee members in mandatory attendance began to sing, in four-part harmony, "(I'll Be with You) In Apple Blossom Time," which was probably the worst thing that has ever happened to me. Shamed beyond recognition, I relinquished my chair and stood the test of time, which I failed miserably.

I left the committee room—but not without first sequestering the still-harmonizing breath-shocked members, a chain and padlock proving more effective by far than any adolescent babysitter—and set forth to seek my fortune.

I hit the road, Jack, hoping to come back more than I was before.

My first stop was the 18th century, but I didn't fit in, so I carried on, back to the dark ages. Boy, were they dark! This time is not for me, I thought, and presently I returned to the present, only to find myself sitting on Santa's lap at Gimbel's (all right, the near present). This Santa was pretty low-rent. He was emaciated, which only drew attention to the oil-soaked rags he used for padding. His breath stank of cheap whiskey and Bermuda onions and he had enormous red bags under his eyes. "And what would you like for Christmas, young man?" Santa asked.

"I'd like to live in a world where people respected each other or, barring that, at the very least respected each other's personal space," I replied.

"Can't help you with that," Santa replied. "How about a candy cane or a magic wand with bonus attachments?"

Clearly, Santa could not give me what I was looking for, so I went looking elsewhere.

On the corner of Thirty-Third and Third I tripped over a wise man. "Watch where you're going, wise guy," said the wise man. "I'm wise to you."

Fortune was smiling on me. A wise man surely had some wisdom to offer.

"Can you offer me any wisdom?" I asked the wise man.

"Sure can," he replied. "How much you got?"

"How much what?" I asked.

He became convulsed with laughter and started foaming at the mouth. "How much what, the wise guy asks! Money, cash, moolah, filthy lucre," he spat, foam flying in all directions.

"I've got three tenners," I told him.

"Thirty bucks? I don't even flash my foreskin for thirty bucks," he replied with a sneer.

"How about thirty bucks and a song?" I offered.

"What song?"

"I can do passable versions of 'Praise the Lord and Pass the Ammunition' and 'A Hot Time in the Old Town,'" I suggested.

"No good," the wise man replied. "A couple of tourists from Bulgaria just did a medley of those two tuneful ditties. Do you know '(I'll Be with You) In Apple Blossom Time'?"

Clearly fate was on my side. I had never heard that song before the committee members had shamed me with it. Now I knew the tune like the back of my hand! "Deal," I said, and began to sing.

"I'll be with you in apple blossom time,
I'll be with you to change your name to mine.
One day in May
I'll come and say:
'Happy the bride that the sun shines on today!'
What a wonderful wedding there will be,
What a wonderful day for you and me
Church bells will chime
You will be mine

In apple blossom time."

"Bravo," the wise man shouted, though he spared me the standing ovation and remained prone. "Here's your wisdom: A rolling stone gathers no moss, so get the fuck out of here." I reluctantly surrendered my thirty bucks and moved on once again.

Clearly, fate was toying with me. Where next? I wondered. Who knows where or when? I sang, softly, to no one in particular.

Perhaps gainful employment is the ticket, I considered.

I started walking uptown. At the corner of Forty-Second and Third I noticed an employment agency. What the hey, I figured, I've got nothing to lose but my dignity.

The receptionist was a knockout. Literally, I learned, a former national women's kick boxing featherweight champ. "Have a seat and a counselor will be out shortly," she cooed in a sultry voice that made me yearn for a kick or two.

While I waited I picked up a magazine, a rather risqué magazine for a business of this sort, I must say, featuring gauzy photos of middle managers of both of the major genders in various states of dishabille. I did, thankfully, find the featured interview quite engaging.

After a while a man in a gray flannel suit emerged from an office. "Who's next in pecking order?" he asked the room. As I was the only one waiting, I replied, "Must be me."

He introduced himself as Greg and shuttled me into his office. "So, what are you looking for?" he asked.

"I'd like to get back on my feet again," I replied. "Almost anything will do for starters."

"Well," he said, "right now we have two openings that might fit the bill. One is for an oyster shucker at a senior center in Moscow, Idaho, and the other is for CEO of a major multinational holding company located just a few short blocks from here."

"The latter, please," I told Greg.

"Excellent," he replied. "And perfect timing. There's a board meeting starting in about ten minutes; you have just enough time to make it and lead the meeting."

He gave me a sheet of paper with the address and wished me good luck. I walked over to the address on the sheet of paper. The building looked eerily familiar. I asked the security guard, who looked decidedly familiar, where the meeting was being held. He told me and I took the elevator to the specified floor, where a receptionist, who looked indubitably familiar, escorted me to an uncannily familiar-looking conference room. As I entered the room I heard familiar music, a cappella, and saw a bunch of gnawingly familiar faces with mouths wide open.

"Church bells will chime
You will be mine
In apple blossom time."

Lost

An old man who has lost his way wanders about, in search of his way and his home. Along the way, he meets an old woman who, in her own way, is also lost. "Old woman, I have lost my way," the old man tells the woman.

"I too have lost my way," the old woman says. "But tell me, old man, have you not lost something else?"

The old man thinks for a moment and then begins to cry. "Yes," he says, "I have lost something else. I have lost a wife."

"Now isn't that a coincidence!" the old woman says. "I am a lost wife. Perhaps we two are lost together."

"Perhaps we have found each other," the old man suggests.

"Perhaps," they say in unison, and together they go in search of their home.

"Not this one," says he.

"Not this one," says she.

They say this of many homes, but not this one. This one, they agree, is their home, as they enter the house, front door unlocked and ajar. And in the living room sits an old woman who says, "Husband, you have returned. But who is this woman?"

The President

Taking his daily constitutional, Walter runs into a woman of the neighborhood, of indeterminate age, who seems to have taken a liking to Walter, and often speaks to him.

"Hello, young man," the woman says, and Walter, as always, wonders if, and by what definition, he may be considered a young man. This time the woman addresses the most recent speech by the president. "Did you see him on the TV last night?" the woman asks. "He's a crook, a liar and a phony," she says. "There hasn't been an honest man in the White House since Wendell Willkie."

Walter smiles, agrees with the woman, and walks on, wondering what it would be like to inhabit a universe in which Wendell Willkie was once president.

Box Sets

As a jazz fanatic, I'm an avid collector of box sets featuring the work of the musicians I most admire. But, for classic jazz recordings in particular, the labels often put out so many overlapping permutations of the material in different packages and formats that it's hard to know which set or sets to buy. I love Clyde Davis' work, and the Swell years represent his finest period, as far as I'm concerned, but where do I even begin when faced with so many choices?

The Complete Clyde Davis on Swell Records

The Complete Clyde Davis on Swell Records (Chuck Vanderpool Remastered Edition)

The Complete Clyde Davis Trio Sessions on Swell Records

The Complete Clyde Davis Trio Sessions on Swell Records (Deluxe Limited Edition)

The Complete Clyde Davis Studio Master Takes on Swell Records

The Complete Clyde Davis Trio Master Takes on Swell Records

The Complete Clyde Davis Live Recordings on Swell Records

Live and in the Studio: Highlights from the Complete Clyde Davis on Swell Records

For Collectors Only: Rarities from the Complete Clyde Davis on Swell Records

Clyde Davis: The Original Mono Recordings on Swell Records

Clydeside: The Complete Clyde Davis Sideman Sessions on Swell Records

The Rematch

After many years, the tortoise and the hare agreed to a rematch. The contest was billed as the race of the millennium. It was the hottest ticket in town, and the aged contestants were guaranteed a cool million apiece for the mile run. And this time the hare wasn't about to make the same mistake as last time. So when the starting pistol sounded, the hare took off at breakneck speed, while the tortoise began to crawl. And it was over in seconds, as the hare, now well over two-thousand years old, collapsed, victim to a heart attack.

"That crazy hare," said the tortoise, "a whole lot older, but not a bit wiser."

The Reunion

The Hear-No-Evil, See-No-Evil and Speak-No-Evil monkeys got together for a reunion. After some small talk, how's the wife and kids, that sort of thing, they compared notes on evil, their common bond. See-No-Evil was the first to speak. He spoke of all the evil he had heard since the monkeys last met. He spoke for hours, so vast was the evil he had heard. Speak-No-Evil listened intently, but somehow Hear-No-Evil didn't hear a thing, in one ear and out the other. Then it was Hear-No-Evil's turn to speak, and he spoke at length of all the evil, all the atrocities, all the pain to which he had been an eyewitness. Speak-No-Evil paid close attention, taking copious mental notes, but See-No-Evil simply could not get a clear picture of the evil that Hear-No-Evil was describing. Finally it was Speak-No-Evil's turn to speak, but he chose to remain silent, knowing that if he spoke it would be more than the other two, each in his own way, could bear.

The Man Who Couldn't
Tie His Shoes

There once was a man who never learned to tie his shoes. He was otherwise extremely smart and capable. In fact, he was a top student all through grade school, high school and college, always the class valedictorian. This man was so brilliant that he got a full scholarship to the most prestigious technical university in the country, where he completed a Ph.D. in nuclear physics in record time. When he was only twenty-two he invented a bomb more powerful than any that had previously existed, a bomb that could kill billions of people cleanly and efficiently without even the slightest damage to property. But still, despite all this, he couldn't tie his shoes.

Thank heaven for loafers.

Hard-Boiled Dick, Second Take

She was the b-side of a brutal murder. A piece of fluff
called Mandy. "That's Mandy with a d," she said two or
three times. She was a centipede—one hundred legs and
each one a work of art. A diamond on every finger—for
protection, she said. She gave me the lowdown, on the
floor. So this is how it is, I thought. Seven thousand names
and as many phone numbers was more than I could handle.
"What's in it for me," I asked. "Nothing more than the joy
of doing a job and doing it well," she said. I was trying to
think of another word for no when she planted a big wet
kiss on my eighty-eights, something like Chopin, but less
Polish. "All right, sister," I said, "I know when I'm licked,
but tell me one thing—why did you do it?" But she just
smiled and started taking her shoes off. All of them.

Syncopated Clock

Morning now. It is morning now. Is morning now. Now. Morning. Now it is morning. Morning. It is morning now. It is now. It is now 10 a.m. It is 10 a.m. Now. 10 a.m., now, it is. Ten in the morning, it is. Ten in the morning, now. Ten. Ten and some seconds, now. It is now 10 a.m. and some seconds. It is now 10:01.

I have an appointment today. An appointment. With somebody. Later. Later today. I have an appointment later today. With somebody. Later. Later today. It is an important appointment. An important appointment with an important person. Later today. Later. At three o'clock. Three o'clock in the afternoon. This afternoon. I have an appointment. I have an appointment this afternoon at three o'clock with an important person. I made the appointment weeks ago. Four weeks ago, to be precise. Four weeks ago. Four weeks ago I made an appointment for three o'clock this afternoon. That was four weeks ago. Four weeks ago to this day. Four weeks ago I made an appointment for three o'clock. For three o'clock today. With an important person. That's in five hours. Five hours from now. It is now ten o'clock. Ten o'clock and a couple of minutes. It is now 10:02.

I must prepare for my appointment. I haven't much time to prepare for my appointment. Hardly any time. Less than five hours. Less than five hours to prepare for my important appointment. Hardly any time. It is after ten o'clock. I have less than five hours to prepare for my appointment. Fewer than five hours. Hardly any time to prepare for my appointment. That's hardly any time. Hardly any time to prepare for an important appointment. To prepare for an appointment of great importance with an important person. Five hours is no time. No time at all. And I have less than five hours. Fewer than five hours. And as time goes on I have even less time. Less than five hours. Fewer than five hours. It is now 10:04.

It is now 10:06, 10:07, 10:08. Time flies. *Tempis fugit.* Time flies when you're having fun. Am I having fun? I don't think I'm having fun. I'm not having fun, yet time is flying. Time flies though I'm not having fun. It is now 10:15, 10:17, 10:19. Time flies. It is now 10:25. It is 10:26 and I have an appointment today. Later today. At three o'clock. At three o'clock I have an appointment with an important person. An important appointment. I must prepare. There is not much time. Hardly enough time. Fewer than five hours. Fewer—that's correct. Fewer is correct; less is not. Fewer than five hours. You can count hours, hence fewer than five hours. Less time than is necessary. Time is a concept, hence less. Not enough time. Not enough. Not enough time, not enough hours. Time flies. It is 10:30. It is 10:30 and there is not enough time. There is never enough time. There are too few hours in a day; too little time. There are two few days in a week; too little time. There are too few weeks in a year; too few. Months? Yes, months, months too few and not far enough between. Scandalous. It is 10:30. Scandalous. Time as we know it is scandalous. Time is reprehensible. Time is anathema. Time flies. It is now 10:30. There is never enough time. Never enough. Too few ticks, too few tocks, it is now 10:30, it is now eleven o'clock. Where did the time go?

It is now 10:30, it is now eleven o'clock. Tick-tock, tick-tock, tick-tock, tick-tock. Can you sing "The Syncopated Clock"? I can.

It is noon. I've been singing "The Syncopated Clock" for an hour. I've been having fun. Time flies when you're singing "The Syncopated Clock." It is noon. I've been singing "The Syncopated Clock" for an hour. It's a damn good tune. A damn catchy tune, "The Syncopated Clock." They don't write tunes like "The Syncopated Clock" anymore. Times have changed. There are too few really catchy tunes being written these days. Scandalous. Scandalous, this lack of catchy tunes. Time flies. It is 12:01. Like sands in the hourglass, it is 12:02.

It is 12:03. It's late, it's late and I have a date at three. An important date. An important appointment with a very important person. A veritable VIP. At three. I have to see a VIP at three. At three, just the two of us, the VIP and me. It's getting late, it's getting late. Later and later. It's getting later and later. It's 12:03:14. You were hoping I didn't have a second hand, weren't you? But I do, I do have a second hand. I bought my watch at a second-hand store. All second-hand watches have second hands. It's true. You can see for yourself. Go hock your watch. Go hock a watch that does not have a second hand. Then after the time limit expires—o cruel time!—go pay a visit to the hock shop. You will see that your watch has sprouted a second hand. It is now 12:03 and fifty-nine seconds. It is now 12:04.

I must prepare. But how? How shall I prepare for my important appointment. Is it possible to properly prepare for an appointment of such great importance? Highly doubtful. Yet I must prepare. It would not do for me to be completely unprepared. Even if I cannot hope to be sufficiently prepared (especially considering the insufficient time I have at my disposal for such preparation), I must nonetheless be somewhat prepared, for partial preparation is at least somewhat preferable to complete and utter lack of preparation, *n'est-ce pas?*

It's 12:05. Perhaps I should open my eyes. That would be a start. A genesis of sorts. A symbolic awakening, you might say. Did I hear someone say a "symbolic awakening?" No, on second thought, I didn't hear someone say, "a symbolic awakening," I heard someone ask if someone said, "a symbolic awakening," that is, I heard it second hand. It is 12:05:02.6. Just kidding! My watch doesn't do tenths. Actually, it's somewhere between 12:05:02 and 12:05:03, or at least it was when I said it was 12:05:02.6, because now it's actually 12:15. My, how time flies.

Resolved, I will open my eyes. I know what you're thinking. You're thinking, if he had his eyes closed all this time, how did he know what time it was, down to the very second, no less? Well, I'll tell you. I've been consulting my internal clock. My internal clock is synchronized with my second-hand watch. That's how. It's 12:16, smarty-pants. It's 12:17. My eyes are open, but nothing looks different. I'm still pressed for time. I'm still pressed for time. I'm still pressed for time. Like sands in the hourglass, I'm still pressed for time. It's 12:30.

Only two and a half hours until my appointment. Less. Fewer than two and a half hours. Because I'd like to be five minutes early. Five minutes is a good amount of time. If I'm five minutes early there's no chance I'll be late, yet I won't be too early either, and thereby appear too eager. Five minutes is the perfect amount of time, the perfect number of minutes. Fewer would be dangerous, more would be risky. So you see I have only two hours and twenty-five minutes. And that's two hours and twenty-five minutes bed to door. It will take me at least fifteen minutes to get there. Perhaps twenty. I should leave myself twenty minutes, just to be on the safe side. If it only takes fifteen minutes to get there, and I arrive five minutes early, that is, ten minutes before the appointment, I can walk around the block a couple of times to kill five minutes and then go up at five minutes of three. Nonetheless, leaving myself twenty minutes travel time in addition to five minutes for early arrival, I really have no more than two hours and five minutes to prepare, or should I say two hours, for it is now 12:35. It's 12:35 and ten seconds and I know what you're thinking. You're thinking, he's going nowhere fast, and pretty slowly at that.

But you're wrong. I'm not going nowhere fast. I'm going somewhere soon. I've got a three o'clock appointment. An appointment at three with a VIP. I must prepare, I must prepare, I must prepare. It is 12:45. What was I doing for the past ten minutes?

It's hard to resist the temptation to sing "The Syncopated Clock" for another hour. It's such a catchy tune. I love that tune. I love "The Syncopated Clock." I love "The Syncopated Clock" as I have never loved another tune. Other tunes have come close—"Time On My Hands," for instance, not to mention that old American favorite, "Grandfather Clock"—but the "Syncopated Clock" is clearly my favorite. I will allow myself another fifteen minutes with "The Syncopated Clock."

It's 1:05. I cheated. I stole another five minutes with "The Syncopated Clock," and even then it was hard to break away. Parting is such sweet sorrow. Every time we say goodbye I die a little. Will I see you in September or lose you to a summer love? It's 1:06. Maybe I'll stretch a little. Just a little stretch. To get started. A morning stretch, as it were. A belated morning stretch, most assuredly, but a morning stretch nonetheless, even if it is after noon. The afternoon. And so, a little morning stretch at 1:07, 1:08, 1:09. Like sands in the hourglass, the morning stretches way past noon.

It is 1:10. In due time I will stretch again, a limb as yet unstretched, perhaps my left leg, or my prick, no, not my prick, that would lead to complications. I cannot afford such complications. I have an important appointment at three o'clock. Leg yes, prick no. It's 1:11. Three ones.

1:12, 1:13, 1:14, left leg. Left leg, but no prick and no "Syncopated Clock." No syncopated cock. No second-hand cock. No internal cock. 1:15.

1:16. Infernal cock! It's that song—I can't stop thinking about that song. For as long as I can remember, "The Syncopated Clock" has always given me a hard-on. A hard-on, a boner, an erection—call it what you will. What? I've never heard that one before! In fact, I can't even begin to fathom the etymology. 1:17.

1:18. I must prepare, I must prepare, I am unprepared, I must not be unprepared. Preparation is called for. Preparation is essential. Readiness is all. To pee or not to pee?

1:21. Back in bed. Nothing like a good long piss to get rid of a hard-on. It makes you wonder. It makes me wonder. I mean, I wonder, was it really the song after all, or was it the need to pee and nothing more? Can one ever be sure? 1:24. Did I tell you I have an appointment at three? An important appointment. A very important appointment. An appointment with a VIP. A very important person. But you knew that. I didn't have to explain, did I? Everybody knows what a VIP is. It's unambiguous. VIP is unambiguous. Like BMOC. Or FBI. Or SOB. VIP is unambiguous. Others are ambiguous. Like SRO. Like NRA. Like NEA. But VIP is unambiguous. Very Important Person. But you knew that.

I forgot to mention—it's 1:30. Time flies. Time is running out. Like sands in the hourglass.

One-thirty, one-thirty, one-thirty. Say it enough and it's 1:35.

I really must prepare. But I don't know where to start, so I'll start with the obvious. I have an important appointment at three o'clock. The importance of this meeting cannot be stressed enough. Why did I use the passive voice? I mean, why was the passive voice used? To be prepared is necessary. An important appointment is scheduled for three o'clock. Time flies. No—I must take personal responsibility for my actions. I fly time! It is two o'clock.

It is two o'clock and I am woefully unprepared. I have an important appointment in one hour. One hour. Sixty minutes. One hour is no time. One hour is no time. One hour is no time. Time is cruel. Time is malicious. Time is vicious. Like a circle. Stop!

It's two o'clock. I hear the ticking of my watch. I see the spasmodic movements of my second hand. I smell trouble. I taste fear. I touch my cock. Stop!

I must prepare. Time is running out. Like sands in the hourglass, like sands in the hourglass, like sands, like syncopated sands in the hourglass, like the days of my life. 2:15. Fear and trembling. Jehovah's Witnesses at my door. Soap operas on the TV. And on the radio the Boston Pops performs "The Syncopated Clock." Stop!

2:15. Gotta get out of bed. Time is running out. I have to leave in twenty minutes. I have to leave in twenty minutes to be sure I'll be there by five minutes of three. To my important appointment. I want to be there five minutes early. I don't want to be late. It's too important. It will take me at least fifteen minutes, possibly twenty. I must leave by 2:35. That's only twenty minutes. I must get out of bed, must get dressed, brush my teeth, comb my hair. I must beat the clock. I must not beat my cock, must not sing "Syncopated Clock." Breakfast would be nice—but no, hardly enough time. 2:16, 2:17, 2:19. Must

get out of bed. Only sixteen minutes. All right—up and at 'em. Is it up and at 'em or up and Adam? Adam or at 'em? At 'em or Adam? I must not sing "Syncopated Clock," must not sing "Syncopated Clock," must not

sing "Syncopated Clock." Pull on clothes. Proper clothes. Proper clothes for very important appointment. Brush teeth. Good—teeth brushed. Comb hair—hair combed, right on schedule. Shit. Stop!

Shitting—I hadn't accounted for shitting. My timetable does not allow for a shit. But I cannot not shit. I can't walk all the way there holding it in. Even if I could last until I got there, and even if I got there five minutes early as I've planned all along, what if the VIP is ready to see me at five of three? It's possible. The VIP might have finished his prior appointment early, or whatever business he'd been attending to, and on seeing me enter the office five minutes early the VIP might say, to himself or perhaps out loud, "Well, as long as he's here five minutes early I might as well see him now. That way I might be able to get out of here five minutes early today." And even if I could hold it in throughout the meeting, my situation would inevitably take its toll on my disposition, not to mention my demeanor, and that could very likely adversely affect the outcome of the meeting. So you see, I must shit. But a quick one. Shit done, ass wiped in record time. It is now 2:19. Stop!

It can't be 2:19. I was still in bed at 2:19. My watch must have stopped. My watch has stopped. The second hand is not moving. Cheap watch! Cheap, second-hand watch. And my internal clock has stopped too. At 2:19. My internal clock was synchronized with my second-hand watch, and when my watch stopped my internal clock stopped. I have to turn on the radio. I have to turn on the news. I have to hope they'll mention the time. "And that's today's top stories. The time is now 2:40." 2:40? That's too late! Much too late. Five minutes too late. I can't go. It's too risky. Even though I've allowed for some extra time, even though I planned to arrive five minutes early, even though I've given myself twenty minutes for the walk, whereas it might only take fifteen, nonetheless, to leave now would be cutting it too close, because what if something else were to happen that I hadn't accounted for, like the shit, what then?

I have to cancel the appointment. I must cancel the appointment. I can't take so many chances. It's no good for my ticker. I must cancel. So I call the VIP. I get his secretary.

"Hello," I say, "I have to cancel my three o'clock appointment with the VIP. Something unexpected came up. I'd like to reschedule. Four weeks from today, same time? Perfect."

Math Problems

1. Johnny wants to buy a bicycle, which costs $200. He has only $120 in his savings account, but he knows of a way to earn the rest of the money he'll need for the bicycle: In his neighborhood there is a man who will pay $15 apiece to have certain individuals bumped off. Johnny goes to see the man, and that day he is given $45 and 3 names. He successfully pulls off all 3 hits, but somehow slips up and leaves a clue. The police catch him and he spends 3 years in a juvenile detention home. When he gets out, he still has the money in his savings account and the $45 hit money, but due to inflation the cost of the bicycle has gone up.

   If the annual rate of inflation is 2.80%, and Johnny has been earning 3.50% interest on his savings account, compounded quarterly, how many more people will he have to kill before he can buy the bicycle?

2. Mr. Smith wants to get from Plainville to Anytown. He can take a train, a bus, or a plane. The plane is the quickest way. The plane will take Mr. Smith from Plainville to Anytown in just under 3 hours. The plane costs $200, one way. The cheapest way to get from Plainville to Anytown is by bus. The bus costs only $35, but it's also the slowest and least comfortable of the 3 choices. The bus takes 24 hours to get from Plainville to Anytown. The train, on the other hand, is relatively comfortable yet still moderately priced. The train costs $75 and gets from Plainville to Anytown in 15 hours. Mr. Smith decides to take the train.

   Mr. Smith kisses his wife in Plainville goodbye. Mr. Smith is going to Anytown to see his other wife. Mr. Smith is a bigamist. Mr. Smith has 2 wives.

Mr. Smith leaves his house in Plainville at 2 p.m. His train leaves at 4 p.m. It takes Mr. Smith 45 minutes to drive from his house to the train station. When he arrives at the train station, Mr. Smith is propositioned by a hooker. Since he has some time to kill, and since he has saved $125 by taking the train instead of a plane, he decides to go with the hooker. They go to the Paradise Motel, which is a 5-minute walk from the station. A room at the Paradise Motel costs $20 for the hour, $25 with clean sheets. Mr. Smith gives the desk clerk a twenty.

Once in the room, the hooker explains her schedule of fees. Her basic rate is $100 for a half hour, with an additional charge of $25 for "Greek," and she doesn't do S&M. Mr. Smith decides to splurge for Greek, since neither of his 2 wives allow him that particular outlet. He gives the hooker $125 and they both strip. The hooker rubs some K-Y on Mr. Smith's cock. A tube of K-Y costs $3.95. After Mr. Smith is through fucking the hooker in the ass he asks her if she'll marry him. The hooker declines.

Mr. Smith stays in the room with the hooker until 3:30, when he decides it's time to start heading back to the station. He gets to the station at 3:35 and discovers that his train will arrive 15 minutes late. When the train arrives, actually 20 minutes late, Mr. Smith boards and settles into a seat.

A short while later, in the café car, Mr. Smith meets Miss Doe. They talk for 25 minutes, after which Miss Doe tells Mr. Smith that she has a sleeper, which costs an extra $50, but 2 can sleep as cheaply as 1 as long as they're discreet. Mr. Smith, never one to pass up a bargain, goes to the sleeper with Miss Doe. They do not sleep.

The train pulls into Anytown the next morning at 7:20 a.m. Mr. Smith takes a cab from the station to his house in Anytown. The cab ride takes 18 minutes and costs $16.45. Mr. Smith gives the cabbie a twenty.

When Mr. Smith enters his house there's nobody home. Mr. Smith finds a note from his wife on the dining room table explaining that she has left him to live with a woman in Plainville.

Where does that leave Mr. Smith?

3. A third-world nation, which we will call Nation X, has a population problem. Nation X is very small in area. Nation X is about the size of Rhode Island, the smallest state in the United States. Nation X has a population of 6,420,000. There is not enough food to go around. There is hardly enough room for the people of Nation X to go around. The people of Nation X are always bumping into each other. The people of Nation X do not practice birth control. The population of Nation X is growing by leaps and bounds. Most of the inhabitants of Nation X are very young. Most of them are also very hungry. The average family in Nation X is a family of 8. There is never enough milk to go around. Most of the children of Nation X are starving. The USA decides to help. They send over a synthetic milk substitute called Pseudo-Moo to feed the babies of Nation X. The USA sends 40 tons of Pseudo-Moo to Nation X. 1 lb. of Pseudo-Moo is enough to make 80 8-oz. glasses of artificial milk. An 8-oz. glass of Pseudo-Moo is enough to nourish a child for 12 hours. There are 3,495,000 babies in Nation X. The USA wants to help. 15 tons of the Pseudo-Moo contain a deadly poison. The poison, when ingested, kills within 30 minutes.

What will the population of Nation X be tomorrow?

4. Jack's mother sends him out to buy a quart of milk, which costs $1.60. She gives him $2 and tells him to bring back 40 cents change. On his way to the market, Jack meets an old man who tries to sell him magic beans. The beans cost 20 cents each, but to work their magic you have to buy 3, the old man tells Jack. Jack gives the old man a dollar and receives 3 beans and 40 cents in change. He gets to the market and realizes he no longer has enough money to buy a quart of milk, so instead he buys a pint, which costs a dollar. On his way home he cooks up a scheme. He returns home and gives his mother the pint of milk and 40 cents. "Here's a quart of milk and 40 cents change," he tells his mother. Jack's mother thanks him and makes a white sauce, the recipe for which calls for 2 cups of milk. Later, when it's time to feed Jack's baby brother, she realizes there is no milk left. So she gives Jack a dollar and tells him to go to the store to buy a pint of milk. Fearing that once his mother sees the pint she'll realize that the previous "quart" was also a pint, Jack kills his baby brother. He convinces his mother that now that baby brother is dead it would be pointless to buy a pint of milk. He tells his mother that he knows of a man who sells magic beans for 20 cents each, and all you need is 3 of them for them to work their magic. "Perhaps we can plant these beans and wish for baby brother to come back to life," Jack tells his mother. His mother decides it might be worth a try. She gives Jack 60 cents and tells him to find the man and buy 3 beans. Jack goes out, walks around the block, pockets the 60 cents and returns home. He gives his mother the 3 beans he had already purchased. They plant the beans and wish for baby brother to come back to life. Nothing happens.

If a pint of milk costs a dollar and 3 useless beans cost 60 cents, what is the value of a human life?

5. A man drives a car at 50 miles per hour. The car gets 17.5 miles per gallon. The man is going from Point A to Point B. Point B is 326 miles from Point A. The car is a convertible. Point B is in another country. The man has just killed his wife. The car is a Buick convertible. The man has blood on his hands. It is 9 p.m. The man has stabbed his wife 6 times in the chest. The car's gas tank holds 20 gallons. The wife's corpse is at Point A. The man has left Point A with a gas tank three-quarters full. Halfway between Point A and Point B is the Sunflower Diner. A hamburger at the Sunflower Diner costs $1.35. A side order of French fries costs 65 cents. A Coke costs 45 cents. When the man in the Buick convertible reaches the Sunflower Diner he decides he'd like a coffee to go. He enters the diner. He orders a coffee to go. Light and sweet. The coffee costs 35 cents. He pays for it and takes it out. He gets into his car again and starts it up. He drives 12 miles, this time at 35 mph, then decides to take a sip of his coffee. There has been a mistake; the coffee is black, no sugar. The man drives back to the Sunflower Diner. He stabs Ethel, the waitress responsible for the coffee mixup. He stabs her 6 times in the chest. He gets back into his car and once again heads toward Point B, this time at 55 mph. He runs out of gas along the way.

Where is he?

6. A man goes to a fancy restaurant and orders a steak dinner. The waiter asks the man whether he'd like the 12-oz. or the 16-oz. steak. "What's the difference?" the man asks.

"The 16-oz. steak is four ounces larger," the waiter replies.

"I know that," the man says, "I mean what's the difference in price?"

"The 16-oz. steak is more expensive," the waiter replies.

"I figured as much," the man says. "How much more?"

"The 16-oz. steak costs $5 more than the 12-oz. steak," the waiter replies.

"All right," the man says, "I'll take the 16-oz. steak."

"Would you like that with a baked potato or sautéed mushrooms?" the waiter asks.

"What's the difference?" the man asks.

"Mushroom is a fungus, potato is a tuber," the waiter replies.

"I know that," the man says. "I mean what's the difference in price?"

"The mushrooms cost $1 extra," the waiter replies.

"All right, I'll take the mushrooms," the man says.

"Would you like your salad with Italian dressing or bleu cheese?" the waiter asks.

"Do I get a salad?" the man asks.

"If you'd like one," the waiter replies, "but it's à la carte."

"How much does it cost?" the man asks.

"All depends," the waiter says.

"On what?" the man asks.

"The dressing," the waiter replies.

"What's the difference?" the man asks.

"The Italian dressing is basically oil and vinegar with herbs and spices, and the bleu cheese is a creamy dressing made with bleu cheese, as the name implies."

"In price!" the man says.

"A salad with Italian dressing is $5. The bleu cheese costs $1 extra," the waiter replies.

"All right, give me the bleu cheese," the man says.

"Will there be anything else?" the waiter asks.

"No," the man says, "that'll be all."

The waiter leaves the man's table. After a while he returns with the man's meal. He has gotten the entire order wrong. He brings the man a 12-oz. steak, a baked potato, and a salad with Italian dressing.

What's the difference?

Communication

"Don't talk to me about communication," he told her.

The Housewife Is in the Kitchen

I

The housewife is in the kitchen preparing dinner. The husband comes home and asks what's for dinner. The housewife says Peking duck. The husband says great I love Peking duck when will it be ready. The housewife says tomorrow.

II

(The Housewife's Side of the Story)

I'm in the kitchen preparing dinner. My husband comes home and asks what's for dinner. I say Peking duck. My husband says great I love Peking duck when will it be ready. I say tomorrow.

III

(The Husband's Side of the Story)

My wife is in the kitchen preparing dinner. I come home and ask what's for dinner. My wife says Peking duck. I say great I love Peking duck when will it be ready. My wife says tomorrow.

IV

(The Duck's Side of the Story)

Quack quack quack quack quack quack quack quack. Quack quack quack quack quack quack quack quack quack. Quack quack quack quack quack. Quack quack quack quack quack quack quack quack quack quack quack quack. Quack quack quack tomorrow.

V

The housewife[1] is in the kitchen[2] preparing dinner[3]. The husband[4] comes home and asks what's for dinner. The housewife says Peking[5] duck[6]. The husband says great I love Peking duck when will it be ready. The housewife says tomorrow.

1. A woman who manages the affairs of her own home.

2. A room specially set apart and equipped for cooking food.

3. The principal meal of the day.

4. A man joined to a woman in lawful wedlock.

5. The former English name of Beijing.

6. Any of various aquatic birds, both wild and domesticated, with short legs, webbed feet, and broad bills.

VI

The woman who manages the affairs of her own home is in the room specially set apart and equipped for cooking food preparing the principal meal of the day. The man joined to the woman in lawful wedlock comes home and asks what's for the principal meal of the day. The woman who manages the affairs of her own home says the former English name of Beijing any of various aquatic birds both wild and domesticated with short legs, webbed feet and broad bills. The man joined to the woman in lawful wedlock says great I love the former English name of Beijing any of various aquatic birds both wild and domesticated with short legs, webbed feet and broad bills when will it be ready. The woman who manages the affairs of her own home says tomorrow.

VII

(The Polish Joke)

The first Pole is in the kitchen preparing dinner. The second Pole comes home and asks what's for dinner. The first Pole says Peking duck. The second Pole says great I love Peking duck when will it be ready. The first Pole says today.

VIII

The duck is in the kitchen preparing dinner. The husband comes home and asks what's for dinner. The duck says housewife. The husband says great I love Peking housewife when will it be ready. The duck says I didn't say Peking housewife I just said housewife.

IX

The husband is in the kitchen preparing dinner. The housewife comes home and asks what's for dinner. The husband says Peking duck. The housewife says great I love Peking duck when will it be ready. The husband relates the following anecdote:

X

The housewife is in the kitchen preparing dinner. The husband comes home and asks what's for dinner. The housewife says Peking duck. The husband says great I love Peking duck when will it be ready. The housewife says tomorrow.

Fighting a Cold

There once was a man who was fighting a cold.

The fight took place at a famous boxing arena in Las Vegas. The man hoped to knock the cold out before he got sick.

Ringside seats for the fight sold for $500 apiece. The boxing fans had never seen a man fight a cold before. This was a big event.

The fight was broadcast on pay-per-view TV, so even if he lost the match the man stood to make lots of money, which is a whole lot better than getting sick for free.

At 8 p.m. it was time for the fight to begin. The opponents took their places in opposite corners. The announcer went to the middle of the ring and spoke into the hanging microphone.

"In this corner, weighing 185 pounds, from Yakima, Washington, Rocky Stillwell," the announcer said as he pointed at the man. The audience cheered wildly.

"And in this corner, weighing, er, almost nothing, from, ahem, from the last person who had the cold, Common Cold Virus!" Most of the audience booed and hissed as the announcer pointed at the virus.

"All right men," the announcer continued, "or should I say man and germ, shake hands and come out fighting."

The man immediately ran over to the announcer and whispered something into his ear. He explained that it would be impossible to shake hands since viruses don't have hands. And even if they did have hands, it wouldn't be fair to have to shake hands with a virus since most colds are actually passed on through hand contact. The announcer thought it over for a minute and said, "All right, just come out fighting."

The two boxers came out into the middle of the ring

and started fighting, though to the audience it looked like there was just one guy punching at nothing. Rocky danced around the ring like Muhammad Ali, jabbing at the air, hoping to knock out the virus. Even if he couldn't see his opponent, he figured he might get lucky. All it would take was one good punch to knock out that puny microbe.

But, alas, this was not to be his lucky night. While Rocky darted around the ring and punched aimlessly, the virus saw an opening and entered his left nostril. Quickly the virus spread throughout Rocky's upper-respiratory system. Almost immediately, Rocky Stillwell, who was no longer well at all, started coughing uncontrollably and sneezing violently. He lost his balance and fell to the mat. He tried to get up again, but he was too weak. Rocky was down for the count. The cold was the winner by a knockout, just one minute into the first round.

As he lay on the mat coughing and sneezing, Rocky decided that the next time he had to fight a cold he would give Vitamin C a try.

Bulimia, Mon Amour

About a month ago, I believe it was on a Tuesday at the crack of dawn, though it could just as easily have been a Thursday during happy hour (a pathologically optimistic appellation if ever there was one), I was unceremoniously exhumed, wholly without preparation, H or otherwise, by a vertiginous little pinprick, a desiccated lasagna monger of the old school, who relentlessly poked and prodded me with an audacious volume of incunabula. "My proposition," he intoned in an elephantine whimper, "I hesitate to use the word 'copulation,' having suffered a Byzantine series of indignities at the hands of an overly randy grandfather clock, hence 'proposition,' though perhaps 'proposal' would be the more fragrant choice, devoid, of course, of any connubial connotations..." (here he paused for emphasis). "My proposal, which is neither voluntary nor mandatory," he clarified with a liberal sprinkling of ghee, "is a matter of mutual corrosion." Upon hearing the word "corrosion," a nostalgic favorite of mine since my brief period in rust removal, I achieved a momentary erection, followed by a spike of interest.

"Just what is it you're trying to say?" I asked in the nonchalant tone of a civil service exam, hoping to mask my hickory-smoked enthusiasm.

"That," he replied, baring a shaved armpit, the left one, "is the crux of the matter. I am proposing nothing less than a matter of mutual corrosion."

He was clearly aware of the effect the word "corrosion" had on me, because he now bared his right armpit, this one abnormally hirsute, as if to make up for the barren landscape of left one. I was suddenly seized by a series of grotesque twitches that turned my face into a veritable Anton Webern composition. Between the twitches I sputtered,

"Tell...me...more!"

"I see I have piqued your interest," he said, as streams of béchamel began to pour from the corners of his mouth. "What I am proposing, should you choose to join me in this quadratic fandango, is—how shall I put it—a partnership of guaranteed corrosion."

He elaborated, but I wasn't listening anymore. I had heard all I needed to hear. I cleared out my bank account and gave him every last cent, a rather pustulant sum, I admit with all due flotsam, but the extent of my legacy nonetheless, a down-payment on our corrosive partnership.

The following day we set up shop in a back alley that had seen better days. I was the front man, while my partner handled the effluvial details. Our first customer was a rather porcine soprano from a minor league opera company in either Decatur or Eau Claire, I wasn't quite sure which, as she had a rather extreme speech impediment, rendering everything she said wholly incomprehensible, her bel canto delivery notwithstanding. However, through an elaborate—and I might add thoroughly corrosive—pantomime, she managed to convey her vestigial needs, which the two of us, each in his own way, satisfied with much aplomb. The rest of the day followed suit. Aspiring divas from every city between fifty and one hundred thousand in population visited us in search of ineffable corrosion, and we gladly—and accurately, I might add—satisfied their every desire. We were quite literally rolling in dough, as my partner insisted on maintaining a concurrent lasagna enterprise.

Tragedy struck, however, on day two. Only minutes after we had completed the estimable incantation for auspicious verisimilitude, an early-morning ritual performed more out of halitosis than temerity, our makeshift hovel was approached by two men in uniform, albeit gender-inappropriate ones. Indeed, the word "men" itself is a stretch, as the first one, attired as a meter maid, was quite a few years short of puberty—I'd have wagered my English toffee on that. The other, a nonagenarian if he was a day, was decked out as an oversized Brownie. They made quite a corrosive pair, I had to admit. The meter maid boy slapped me with a summons that I could make neither cheddar nor tallow of, as it was written in Sanskrit. The ancient Brownie man, a paleolinguist of some esteem, it turned out, marinated the situation and explained the charges in a high, raspy voice reminiscent of radio interference. "It appears, Hon, that you and your shadow have been practicing corrosion without an agent, an offense in explicit contravention of the Geneva Convention. I'm afraid it's our soluble duty to put an end to your intractable omelet and haul your ham hocks off to the pokey."

Mother of sea slugs, I had been duped! The lasagna monger had given his swollen gland that everything was above board, and now I discovered it was all stuffed derma. I was about to demand the return of my misbegotten dowry from my corrosive partner when he pulled a fast one, overturning several vats of hot lasagna as he made his getaway. I managed to sidestep the volcanic pasta, but the other two were not so lucky. Slipping into the molten lasagna sludge, they gripped each other for dear life as they met their respective makers in a touchingly corrosive embrace.

As for me, I was broke, but I was alive, and that was how I liked it. I walked away from the alley of the shadow of lasagna that morning, head cheese held high, toward the nearest men's shelter, and I've never looked back.

Composition in White and Red

All of a sudden he started spitting blood. Deep red liquid. Onto the white sheet. Red on white. Gushing. Cascading over his lips. His chin. Deep red liquid onto the white sheet. Covering the sheet. Red on white. Deep red liquid gushing from his mouth. Covering more of the sheet. Red displacing white. Spreading. Deep red liquid spreading on the white sheet. Blood gushing from his mouth. Covering the sheet. More red. Less white. Drips. Spurts. Flows. Red displacing white. More red, less white. Blood, flowing from his mouth. Onto the white sheet. Sheet almost covered with blood. Less white. Red sheet, patches of white. Blood. Deep red liquid. From his mouth. Onto the sheet. Filling in the white spaces. Deep red sheet, spots of white. Spitting blood. Mouth. Gushes, flows, spurts, drips. Deep red liquid. Replacing all traces of white. Red sheet.

Mr. Mondrian's Confusion

A former Mr. Mondrian, three-time winner of the Mr. Mondrian pageant (a Mondrian look-alike contest (not Mondrian the painter but rather the paintings of Mondrian ("The title Mr. Mondrian is bestowed upon the man who looks most like a painting by Mondrian, the man whose physical form most embodies the essence of Mondrian's work. Mr. Mondrian symbolizes balance and a certain kind of truth...")) (the pageant was, and continues to be, sponsored by The Friends of Mondrian, some of whom were actually friends of the late painter himself, others merely (the word "merely" hardly seems appropriate) champions of the painter's work ("champion" an understatement, to say the least—I have seen Friends of Mondrian burst into tears during the singing of the pageant's theme song, "Behold, Mr. Mondrian"))), at once lost in senility and an Oriental laundromat, a maze of noisy machines (washers, dryers, extractors) and piles of dirty laundry thrown helter-skelter, stumbles, becomes upset and confused (it is too much for him to bear, he who had once been composition personified), and begins to lash out, screaming, kicking machines, overturning laundry carts, shouting obscenities (the din only exacerbated by the Chinese voices raised in response), and, as his rampage gains momentum (he is now pummeling a double-load Bendix with his bare fists), The Friends of Abstract Expressionism crown him Mr. Pollock, symbol of something altogether different.

The Man Who Got Away with It

There once was a man who robbed a bank and got away with it. But he wasn't happy about it. No, he wasn't happy at all. He felt guilty, and he was afraid.

He felt guilty because he knew it was wrong to steal, and he was afraid because he knew he'd be caught. Nobody robs a bank and gets away with it; maybe in the movies, but not in real life. He knew the police would catch him, and then he'd be sent to jail. He was afraid of jail. Life became utter misery for this man. Every time he heard a police siren he was sure they were coming to get him. He became a nervous wreck. He was shaking all the time and he had trouble sleeping.

Finally it became too much for the man to bear. He decided he had to turn himself in. He knew he would find no peace unless he confessed his crime.

So the man went to the bank to make his confession.

He walked up to the receptionist and said, "I would like to see the president of the bank."

"The president only sees people by appointment," the receptionist said. "Do you have an appointment?"

"No, I do not have an appointment," the man said, "but I must see the president because I have robbed this bank and I must confess."

"I see," said the receptionist, and she called the president's office. "Excuse me sir," she said into the phone, "there's a man to see you who claims he robbed this bank."

"Send him in," replied the president.

"Second door to your left," the receptionist said and pointed the man toward the president's office.

The man entered the president's office. "Have a seat," the president said, and the man sat down.

"Now am I to understand you claim to have robbed this

bank?" the president asked.

"Y-y-y-yes," the man answered nervously.

"But I've had no report of any bank robbery," the president said. "Surely I would know if my own bank had been robbed!"

"Nobody knows I did it but me!" the man said, and then he burst out crying. The president handed him a Kleenex.

"I don't understand," the president said.

The man composed himself. "You see," he said, "I was here the other day to make a deposit to my account, and when I was finished filling out the deposit slip I put the pen in my pocket. I know I shouldn't have done it! I don't know what came over me!" And he began crying again. Then he took a pen out of his pocket and handed it to the president. "Here it is," he said. It was a cheap plastic ballpoint pen on which were printed the following words: Property of Third National Bank. "I suppose you'll have to call the police now," the man said.

"Oh, I don't think that will be necessary," the president said, "as long as you promise never to do it again."

"I promise, I promise," the man said gratefully.

"Very well, we'll leave it at that," said the president. "Now did I hear you say you have an account with our bank?"

"Yes I do," the man replied.

"Well, then," the president said, "to show our appreciation for your business, I'd like to give you a little gift." And he handed the man a small, oblong box.

The man opened the box. Inside was a bright, shiny fountain pen on which were engraved the following words: Thank You!

The Ill-Tempered Caviller

1.   The Ill-Tempered Caviller. They don't call him that for nothing. He's a hotheaded motherfucker, a nasty sonofabitch. And he knows it.

2.   Trouble is his middle name. Ill-Tempered is his first name. Caviller is his last name. Everywhere he goes he makes trouble. He's always getting into fights. He can't get along with anyone. He can't help it. But he hates the way he is. He really does hate the way he is. But he can't help it. Someday you're going to kill someone, the Ill-Tempered Caviller tells himself.

3.   The Ill-Tempered Caviller argues with the old ladies in his building, he argues with the guys at work. He argues with the cop on the beat, the candy store owner, cab drivers, bus drivers, subway conductors. He argues with anybody and everybody, regardless of race, color or creed.

4.   Something or other happens that leads some guy to call the Ill-Tempered Caviller a nasty sonofabitch. The Caviller is about to sock the guy in the jaw, but then decides the punk's not worth it. Instead he says, I have certain unalienable rights, one of them being the right to be myself. He pauses for a few seconds. Then he socks the guy in the jaw.

5.   The Ill-Tempered Caviller gets his electric bill. He decides it's too high. So he makes a call to the electric company. A woman answers the phone. For five minutes he screams at her and calls her names, the nicest one being stupid bitch. The woman breaks down and cries. The Caviller hangs up on her, slams the phone real hard. Then he calls the phone company and does the same thing. Even though he hasn't yet received his phone bill.

6.   The high-echelon Nazis were lovers of great art and the Ill-Tempered Caviller loves Mozart. He goes to a concert where they're doing Mozart's *Piano Concerto in C Major, K. 467*. During the andante, some joker in front of the Caviller starts coughing. The Caviller leans forward and whispers in the guy's ear, stop coughing. From the tone of his voice it is clear that he means business. But the guy can't help himself, and he coughs several more times throughout the piece. During the intermission, the Caviller follows the guy to the men's room, where he roughs him up a bit, just enough to teach him a lesson. Next time you feel like coughing, the Caviller tells the guy, go hear some Tchaikovsky.

7.   An old lady comes up to the Ill-Tempered Caviller and asks him to help her cross the street. I can't, I'm in a rush, he says. I'm afraid to cross alone, the old lady says, and adds, it'll only take a second. OK, but you'll have to keep up with me, the Caviller says. He grabs her by the hand and starts to make a mad dash across the street, dragging the old lady behind him. Stop, stop, she screams, you're hurting me. So the Caviller lets go of her, abandons her in the middle of the street, and continues on alone.

8.   The Ill-Tempered Caviller decides to run for office. He runs as an independent. On the campaign trail the Caviller eats hot dogs and kisses babies. One of the babies drools on him. The Ill-Tempered Caviller spits back.

9.   The Ill-Tempered Caviller calls up a radio talk show. He makes a point. The talk show host agrees with him. So the Caviller makes an about-face and takes the other side. The talk show host calls him contentious. The Caviller calls the talk show host an asshole. When he hears himself back on the seven-second delay, the word asshole is replaced by a boop. The Caviller calls the talk show host

a chickenshit faggot for booping him. The talk show host hangs up on him. On the radio the Caviller hears an extended boop followed by a click.

10.   The Ill-Tempered Caviller is pissed. Nobody hangs up on the Ill-Tempered Caviller and gets away with it. He's flushed with anger, convulsed with rage. He feels like a pressure cooker about to explode. He decides to take a drive to blow off some steam.

11.   The Ill-Tempered Caviller gets into a car accident. The driver of the other car is also ill-tempered. Not surprisingly, they get into a fight. Fisticuffs. The Caviller pins the other guy to the side of his car, the other guy's car, that is, and lets out with a barrage of savage blows to the guy's face. The guy's head goes through the window. Shattered glass. The guy's unconscious. Probably dead. The Caviller gets back into his car and speeds away.

12.   There are no secrets, no mysteries, the Ill-Tempered Caviller tells himself.

Fifty Ways To Leave Your Liver

There must be fifty ways to leave your liver, but I can only think of a few. You could leave your liver to your lover, but better your lover shouldn't need your liver. Or you could drink so much that your liver leaves you. Only time will tell whether your lover leaves before your liver. Or, you could leave your liver, with or without onions, on the plate, because you're not really hungry. Besides, you never really cared for liver anyway.

Dear Mrs. Inkwell,

It's over. It's over. It's over. How many times do I have to tell you it's over? I wish I could penetrate your thick skull as easily as—oh never mind. From your last letter I was able to deduce that you still carry the torch ("Darling, you're a cruel bastard, but I still carry the torch," page 17). Well, drop it. That week in Miami Beach was just a lark. Every day I spent with you was the worst day of my life. I was not cut out to be a gigolo. The way you fondled me at the Light Opera of Coconut Grove was unpardonable. I'm not that kind of boy. I thought I was, but I'm not. I should have stayed in Cincinnati. I may have been bored, but at least I could hold my head up high. With you, I learned how to lie. Remember how I complimented your cooking? Well fasten your seat belt, the truth is your meat loaf was the pits, equaled only by your abominable pot roast. I assure you, Mrs. Inkwell, I am cruel only to be kind, and if you had the slightest shred of literacy you'd recognize the reference. Leave me alone! Abandon your cockamamie plan to follow me to Bangalore, you'll only be wasting your time—you'd look lousy in a sari, and anyway, I leave tomorrow for parts unknown. Please pick on somebody your own age.

Sincerely,
Harvey Nudelman

The Man Who Couldn't Spell Cat

There once was a man who couldn't spell cat. He was a perfectly good speller otherwise, but for some reason he couldn't spell cat. Not only could he spell dog, he could also spell Siamese, Cheshire, black, and kitten. But he couldn't spell cat. So when he wanted to write "Siamese cat" he'd end up with "Siamese cheese" or "Siamese nutcracker." He knew it was bad luck for a black cat to cross his path, but he couldn't write "black cat." Sometimes it came out "black hat," which was close but confusing, or "black elephant" which was bad in a different way. Sometimes he'd resort to tricks, like writing "grown-up kitten" instead of "cat."

You'd think that not being able to spell one little three-letter word wouldn't be the worst thing in the world, but it drove this man crazy. I don't get it, he thought. I was the spelling bee champ in fifth grade. I spelled "triskaidekaphobia," which means fear of the number thirteen. If I can spell triskaidekaphobia, why can't I spell cat?

Finally, the man was so upset over his inability to spell cat that he went to see a psychiatrist. "Doctor, doctor," the man said, "you've got to help me. I can't spell cat."

So the psychiatrist accepted the man as his patient. The man went to the doctor twice a week, for an hour at a time. He'd lie on the psychiatrist's couch and talk about his childhood, his fears, and his dreams. This went on for years, and the man paid the psychiatrist thousands of dollars. But there was no breakthrough. No matter how long he stayed in analysis he still couldn't spell cat.

After fifteen years even the psychiatrist was frustrated. "I've never had had such a stubborn case in my entire career," the doctor said. "I've tried everything in my power to help you, but I've failed. Either I'm a bad psychiatrist or you're a stupid idiot." Then the psychiatrist pointed his finger at the man and started yelling, "Yes, yes, that's it! You're a stupid idiot! You can't even spell a simple word like cat. C-a-t! C-a-t! C-a-t!"

"C-a-t?" the man said. "Thanks, Doc. I'm cured!"

The Man in Mama's Bedroom

Mr. Przybylinski lives in the bedroom with Mama. Mama says this is only temporary, but Mr. Przybylinski has been living there for over a year. Mr. Przybylinski is old and smells bad. He don't talk very much. Mr. Przybylinski never goes out. The only time he leaves Mama's room is to go to the bathroom. Whenever I ask Mama why she lets Mr. Przybylinski stay in the room with her she says, "Because the poor man needs a place to stay."

I don't like Mr. Przybylinski and I don't think he likes me either. Mr. Przybylinski don't talk to me much. And when he does he always calls me Girlie. "You shouldn't come in here and bother an old man, Girlie."

"I didn't come here to bother you," I say, but he just turns around and don't even look at me.

"Why does Mr. Przybylinski hate me?" I asked Mama once. "He doesn't hate you, silly, that's just his way," she told me. I don't care if that's his way. I just wish he'd leave.

Mr. Przybylinski eats funny food. All he eats is this mushed-up stuff with hot milk on it. Mama says it's because his teeth ain't so good. He makes funny noises when he eats this mushed-up stuff. It sounds sorta like a garbage truck.

I saw Mr. Przybylinski's pecker once. It was really ugly. I came in the room and he had his pants off and his ugly pecker was hanging down and when he saw me there he said to me, "Go away, Girlie, before I hit you." I went in the kitchen where Mama was and I told her that I saw Mr. Przybylinski's ugly pecker and what he said to me and she said, "You caught him at a bad time."

Mr. Przybylinski sleeps in the same bed with Mama, just like Daddy used to. Daddy didn't call me Girlie, though, he called me Princess.

"Do you love Mr. Przybylinski like you used to love Daddy?" I asked Mama. "Don't be silly," she said.

I asked Mama once why Mr. Przybylinski don't ever go out. "He's a sick man," she told me. "He has a disease which makes him unable to go out."

"Does he pay us rent?" I asked. "Of course not," she said, "he hasn't got any money." And then I said, "But Mr. Schultz would kick us out if we didn't pay the rent."

"That's different," she said. "He's a landlord. We're Good Samaritans."

I don't want to be a Good Samaritan. I want to be a landlord. That way I could kick Mr. Przybylinski out because he don't pay no rent.

I once asked Mama if Mr. Przybylinski has any friends. "We're his friends," she said.

I already said that Mr. Przybylinski smells bad, but sometimes he smells worse than others. That time I saw his ugly pecker he smelled real bad. "How can you sleep in the same bed with that smell?" I once asked Mama. "You get used to it," she said.

Mr. Przybylinski don't bother me, that's one good thing. Like I said, he always stays in Mama's room, except to go to the bathroom.

Do you want to hear about the day that Mama brought Mr. Przybylinski home? It was about a year and a month ago. I remember the day exactly. It was August 14th. I remember because the day before was August 13th, which would have been Daddy's birthday. Daddy died three years ago. He had cancer. He looked terrible before he died. I saw him when he was dead too, in his coffin, and he looked terrible then. His birthday was on August 13th, and last August 13th Mama said to me, "Do you know what day it is?" And I said, "Yes, it's Daddy's birthday." So that's how I remember it was August 14th when Mama brought Mr. Przybylinski home.

I was sitting in the living room watching TV. I heard the door open and I saw Mama and I said, "Hi Mama," and then I saw that she had someone with her. It was Mr. Przybylinski, but I didn't know it then. "Hi honey, we have a guest," she said.

Mr. Przybylinski looked terrible. He was all dirty and he smelled horrible. I said hello to him, but he didn't say nothing to me. "This is Mr. Przybylinski," Mama said to me. "He's going to be staying with us for a little while." "How come?" I said. "Because he's sick and he needs a place to stay," Mama said.

Mr. Przybylinski just sat there smelling bad, not saying a thing. I wasn't thrilled about him staying with us because I didn't think he was very friendly. Mama brought him a glass of juice and he made a lot of noise when he drank it. Then he started talking.

"Please, I must go," he said. "I'll hear nothing of it," Mama said. "You're ill and you need someone to take care of you." Then Mr. Przybylinski said, "No, this is not right." But Mama said, "You're staying with us, and that's that." Then she took him in the bathroom and washed him. After that she took him in the bedroom, and he hasn't left it for over a year except, like I said, to go to the bathroom.

Mr. Przybylinski is crazy. He never watches TV. He listens to the radio a lot, though. He listens to funny Polish music. Sometimes I pass by the room and he's dancin', but when he sees that I'm there he stops. "What are you looking at, Girlie?" he says. "Nothin'," I say.

I once tried to make friends with Mr. Przybylinski. No kidding, I really did. I once passed by Mama's bedroom and I saw Mr. Przybylinski crying. Mama wasn't home. She was out shopping. I went in the room and asked him what was the matter and was there anything I could do for him. But he just got up and went over to the window and said, "Go away, Girlie."

Mr. Przybylinski cries a lot, but I don't care no more. I tried to be his friend once, but he didn't want me to, so now I don't care if he cries.

Mama cries sometimes too. I feel real bad when she cries and I go over to her and put my arms around her and say, "Mama, why are you crying?" And she says, "I'm just being foolish." And I say to her, "Please Mama, don't cry," and pretty soon she stops.

Maybe Mr. Przybylinski ain't so bad after all. Mama always says we ought to have compassion for those less fortunate than ourselves. It took me an awful long time to learn how to say Mr. Przybylinski's name. I still ain't sure I got it right.

The Famous Writer

I was returning home from my walk the other morning when I ran into a writer I know only marginally, a writer much more famous than me, who has lived in the neighborhood for many years. He greeted me as if we were the oldest and dearest of friends, which I found odd, as I had always found him rather standoffish when I had met him through mutual friends, both writers who are somewhat more famous than me but less famous than him. "I loved your last book," he told me. I was kind of flattered that this famous writer, even if I found him to be something of a snob and quite full of himself, had enjoyed *Autobiography Without Words*. He then went on to tell me all the things he liked about my book, but it was very disconcerting, as he wasn't describing my book at all. Then I realized that he was describing his own most recent book, which I had read several months ago. I don't know if he was pulling my leg or had become delusional, but I didn't set him straight. I thanked him for his kind words and we parted. I plan to ask him for a blurb for my next book.

A Character

There once was a man who wanted to be a character in a story. It had always been his dream to be a character in a story—not just any character, the *main* character—but nobody ever wrote a story about him. Finally, one day, he decided he had to take the bull by the horns. He couldn't just sit around and wait for somebody to write a story about him.

The man, whose name was Tom, had a friend who was a writer. His friend's name was Peter Cherches, and Peter Cherches was always writing stories about all kinds of people. Tom decided to call Peter Cherches.

"Hey Pete, it's Tom," Tom said when Peter Cherches picked up the phone.

"Hi Tom," said Peter Cherches. "What's up?"

"Pete," Tom said, "I want you to write a story about me."

"I don't know about that, Tom," replied Peter Cherches. "Most of the people I write about are unusual, or at least interesting. I'm sorry to say it, but you're a pretty boring guy."

"I am *not* boring!" Tom protested.

"All right, then, tell me something interesting about yourself that I can write about," Peter Cherches said to Tom.

"Well," said Tom, "I love hot dogs."

"So?" said Peter Cherches. "What's so interesting about that?"

"Yeah, but I *really* love hot dogs," Tom replied. "I eat hot dogs every day."

"An improper diet does not a story make," said Peter Cherches. "Is there anything else?"

"Well, my job is pretty interesting," said Tom. "As you know, I'm an accountant."

"I don't think my readers are interested in accountants," Peter Cherches replied.

"All right then, you could write about the time I broke my leg," Tom said.

"How did you break your leg?" Peter Cherches asked.

"I was skiing," Tom replied.

"And?"

"And what?"

"So, you broke your leg skiing," Peter Cherches said. "What's the rest of the story?"

"Isn't that enough?"

"Listen Tom," said Peter Cherches. "I don't want to be rude, but you're really wasting my time. There's no way I'm going to write a story about you."

All of a sudden Tom's tone of voice changed. "You'll be sorry, Cherches," he said menacingly. "I'll get you for this. I don't know how, and I don't know when, but I'm gonna get you." Then he hung up on Peter Cherches.

Peter Cherches was more than a little worried. Maybe Tom was a strange one after all. Maybe he really was dangerous.

Well, he may have been scared out of his wits, but there was no way Peter Cherches was going to give in and write a story about Tom.

He did have his standards, after all.

Nothing Changes

He couldn't see what she was seeing, yet they were looking at the same thing. She couldn't see how he couldn't see
what she was seeing, when they were looking at the same
thing. "Are you looking at the same thing that I'm looking
at?" she asked him.

"Yes," he said.

"Do you see what I see?" she asked.

"I don't know," he said. "What do you see?"

"I see what you don't see," she said angrily.

"Then I guess I don't see what you're seeing," he replied.

There—he admitted it—he couldn't see what she was
seeing. Nothing changes, she told herself. You live with a
man for twenty-five years and nothing changes.

Feelings

"How are you feeling?" she asked him, in a tone of voice she might use for someone she cared for.

Check-Out Time

The clinging lingerers were impervious to the character-istic hotel smell, a subtle blend of house dick, ammonia, mildew, and room service, for they had successfully tran-scended the olfactory plane of the here and now, now revel-ing in the temporary absence of the potential odors of the near hereafter, 1 p.m., to be precise, mandatory check-out time. Testing the limits of the temporal, and notions there-of, they immobilized perilously toward the aforementioned witching hour, in a brazen attempt to get their money's worth, some might say, not to mention a determined wal-low in the vastly underrated pleasures of static flesh, and the exquisite odors of not dressing, not parting, not saying goodbye.

Phone Sex

I called the phone sex line. "Hello, phone sex line," the voice on the other end said—a sultry, sexy, breathy voice. I was hooked from the git-go.

"Talk dirty to me," I said.

"I think you must be mistaken," the voice (oh, that voice!) replied. "This is the phone sex line!"

"Yes, I know! So go ahead, talk dirty to me."

"A gentleman says please."

"Please talk dirty to me."

"Who do you think you are, mister? This is the phone sex line!"

"Yes, that's why I called. I want phone sex!"

"Hey, don't talk dirty to me, buster," she shot back, this time in a voice that was gravelly, gruff, and shrill. Then, without giving me a chance to respond, she unceremoniously ended the call.

I kept the phone to my ear, wondering if I could get any mileage from the silence.

Takeout

On my way home from work I stop off at the Chinese takeout, halfway between the subway station and my apartment building, where I pick up a small subgum lo mein for myself and a number 5 combination plate: barbecued spare ribs, roast pork fried rice, egg roll and wonton soup, for my prisoner. When I get upstairs I unchain my prisoner and we sit down at the dinner table.

"Is that all you're having?" my prisoner asks.

"Yes," I reply, "I'm not very hungry tonight."

I start eating straight out of the container with chopsticks as my prisoner eats his soup out of its container with a plastic spoon.

"How was work today?" my prisoner asks.

"Same as always," I reply.

"Bullshit, bullshit, bullshit!" he says.

"You got it," I say. "How was your day?"

"Not bad at all," he replies. "I had memories. From before."

"Before here, you mean?"

"Yes, before I was your prisoner. I remember the sad times as well as the happy ones, but that's what life's all about, right? You have to take the sad with the happy."

"Are you sad here?" I ask.

"Well, I wouldn't say I'm happy," he says. "I mean, sure, things could be worse. I do have my memories to keep me occupied."

"Do you ever remember the early days here?"

"No. Only before here."

"Not even the beginning? Not even six years ago?"

"Well, I do remember the day you captured me. I remember how much I hated the first time you chained me, for instance, but I got used to it."

"Yeah, I'm sorry I have to chain you, but I'm sure you must understand."

"Oh yes," he says, "I understand why you have to chain me. And gag me. And I've gotten used to it. But I certainly don't like it."

"You prefer it like this, when the chains are off and the gag is out?"

"Well, sure, of course, who wouldn't?"

"Do you find me abhorrent?"

"I did at first, but you always bring me what I like best from Ho Ting Kitchen, so I always forgive."

I'm relieved. I certainly don't want my prisoner to hate me.

We finish dinner and retire to the living room sofa to watch a film on TCM. It's *It's a Mad, Mad, Mad, Mad World*. My prisoner and I have watched it every time it's been shown on TCM since I captured him, at least twice a year. If not every time it's been shown, at least every time we were aware it was being shown. My prisoner and I love *It's a Mad, Mad, Mad, Mad World*. We crack up every time we watch it, always in the same places. He has a particular fondness for Dick Shawn's antics, and I love how Ethel Merman turns her loud, obnoxious personality into comedic gold.

"Well, it's getting a bit late," I tell my prisoner as the closing credits roll. "Time to get some shuteye."

"Yes, good idea," my prisoner says.

"Why don't you go first," I tell him, as I do every evening.

"All right, thanks," he says, as he does every evening, and he goes to the bathroom to wash up, brush his teeth and pee. When he's done I get the chain and the gag and prepare him for the night.

I go to bed, fall asleep within minutes, and have a nightmare about my own time as a prisoner, which I somehow always manage to forget about during waking hours.

In the morning, I shower, shave and dress. Then I unlock my prisoner again and remove the gag so he can do his morning ablutions. After that, as usual, I serve him a hearty breakfast, which will have to suffice until dinner.

"Sorry I have to do this, pal," I tell him as I chain him to the radiator once again.

"Have a good day at work," he tells me, just before I stuff the gag back in his mouth.

The Wrong Side of the Bed

I woke up on the wrong side of the bed, which was a problem, since it was the side that abuts the wall separating my apartment from the one next door. I rubbed my eyes and saw that I was standing in my neighbor's living room in my PJs.

I don't have much to do with my neighbor. We had a contretemps years ago about the volume of my music, and it's been a cold, uncomfortable non-relationship ever since. When we run into each other we give each other a perfunctory nod.

"What the hell are you doing here?" my neighbor asked. He was wearing a red velvet bathrobe, which somehow didn't surprise me.

"It wasn't my intention to be here," I said. "I must have woke up on the wrong side of the bed."

I looked and saw no opening in the wall that I might have come through.

"That's a ridiculous excuse," he said. "Now I'm going to have to change my locks."

"But I didn't come through the door," I protested.

"Then I'll need to put gates on my windows."

"But I didn't come through a window."

"Well, I'm certainly not moving," he said, huffy.

"Who's asking you to move?"

"Well, what am I supposed to do?"

I figured I'd just leave by the door and go back to my apartment, but I quickly realized that I didn't have my keys, my wallet, or my phone.

"Let me try to find my way back to my bed," I said.

"What the hell are you talking about?"

"Well," I said, "if I got here by waking up on the wrong side of the bed, I need to get back to the wrong side before

I can get to the right side."

"How do you intend to do that?"

"I need to find the place in the wall I must have come through."

"But there's no hole in the wall!"

"It must be some kind of virtual hole," I suggested. "What other explanation can there be?"

"I think you're full of shit," he said, "but go ahead and see if you can find this hole of yours."

I went to the wall and started feeling around. Stood with my back to the wall and moved side to side, up and down. Nothing was happening, all solid wall. But I wasn't ready to give up, so I kept moving around the wall, sometimes with my back flat against it, sometimes facing it with my hands out, sometimes leaning in with my shoulder, and after about five or so minutes something just gave all of a sudden and I was back in bed. Back in bed, but not alone. Asleep on top of the bedding was my upstairs neighbor in his pajamas, blue with little black anchors.

I hardly know my upstairs neighbor. He's an older man, pushing 80, and from my brief encounters with him in the elevator or the hallway he seems like a pleasant guy. How my upstairs neighbor landed on top of my bed I don't know; there was certainly no hole in my ceiling. Anyway, my upstairs neighbor was snoring loudly with a beatific smile on his face. Not wanting to disturb his slumber, I carefully got out of bed, got dressed, and went to the coffee place down the block, where I wrote this on my tablet.

An Auntie Story

Auntie tells us a story. Nobody wants to hear a story, but Auntie tells one anyway. Auntie, we say, nobody wants to hear a story, but she tells it anyway. We are not interested in hearing any story, Auntie, we say, we're not interested in hearing any story of yours or anybody else's, we say, so why do you insist on telling us a story, Auntie. Because, she says, because this is my story, she says, this is my story and I must tell it.

Why don't ya keep it to yaself ya bitch, Father says, why don't ya keep it to yaself, he says, Father, who has never much cared for Auntie, who has heard her stories often enough before, who has never much cared for her stories, he is not alone, we have all heard Auntie's stories often enough before, we have all never much cared for her stories, though not all of us have never much cared for Auntie, some of us have cared very much for Auntie, though not for her stories, we have told her this, we believe that honesty is the best policy.

I *am* my stories, Auntie says, I am my stories and if you don't like my stories you don't like me because my stories are me and if you don't like my stories that means you don't like me. Nobody likes me. You all hate me. You all hate me and you wish I were dead. No we don't, we all say, all of us that is except for Father who says nothing and does hate her and does wish she were dead and so does not protest though the rest of us do because, while we most certainly do not like her stories, we do not dislike Auntie and most certainly do not wish her dead, so we all say, all of us, that is, except for Father, of course, we say, no we don't. Yes you do, she says. No we don't   yes you do   no we don't   yes you do   no we don't   yes you do   no we don't.

All right then, she says, if you don't then I can and I will.

And she does.

Auntie tells us a story. Once upon a time there was an Auntie who was hated by her family. Her family hated her and they wished she were dead. They hated her and they hated her stories. They hated her stories and they hated her. They hated her and they wished she were dead so she couldn't tell her stories any more. They knew that if she were dead she couldn't tell her stories any more because dead people tell no tales, so they wished she were dead because they didn't want to hear her stories any more. And this Auntie knew that her family wished her dead, she knew that they didn't want to hear her stories, they told her that much, and though they never actually told her that they wished her dead, she knew they did. It was obvious. They hated her stories and her stories were her, so if they hated her stories they must have hated her. Yes, they hated her and they wished she were dead. But why do they hate me, she wondered, this Auntie, why do they hate me and why do they hate my stories, they're such wonderful stories, why do they hate my wonderful stories. She wondered why they hated her wonderful stories. And she asked them, the family, she asked them, why do you hate my wonderful stories?

Because your stories are you, Father says.

The Human Mind

"The human mind is like an attic," he told her.

"Yes, I know," she replied. "And I wish you'd get your junk out of mine."

The Man Who Wasn't

There once was a man who wasn't. He wanted to be, but he wasn't. He wished he were, but he wasn't.

I want to be, he thought, but, alas, it was not to be, being—he simply wasn't, and whether he was prepared to face it or not, he wasn't going to be.

Yet he was able to conceive of being, wasn't he? So doesn't that mean he was, after all?

He was and he wasn't.

A Short Nap

I was hired to keep an eye on them. I was hired to watch them, to listen to them. They hired me. He hired me to watch her. She hired me to watch him. They hired me to watch each other.

I'm no detective. I'm no dick, no shamus. Just a guy who needed a job.

I didn't ask any questions. He approached me first and I didn't ask any questions. I didn't ask any questions when she approached me, after him. You just don't ask questions.

He approached me first. He explained the whole thing and there was nothing to explain. Just keep an eye on her and don't ask any questions. Don't make any judgments, don't come to any conclusions, just keep an eye on her.

She said the same thing, only in different words. Just keep an eye on him and don't ask any questions. Just keep an eye on him and don't make any judgments, don't bother with conclusions.

Will do, I said. Will do, I told him. Will do, I told her. And don't worry, I told them both, so they wouldn't worry.

He approached first, she approached next. Keep an eye on her, keep an eye on him. Will do, will do.

It was a job. That's all it was to me. A job. Money. Cash up front. More to come. If I did a good job. A good job. Whatever that meant.

We discussed money. I discussed money with him first. There wasn't much to say. I told him what I wanted. He told me what he had. I told him what I needed. He told me what he'd give me. I told him I'd take it.

I discussed money with her next. We talked figures. I told her I liked hers. She told me I was fresh. I told her what I wanted. She told me I couldn't have it. I told her what I needed. She told me what she'd give me. I told her

I'd take it.

I took it. I took it from her, I took it from him. I've been taking it for years, from all sides.

Look, it was a job. That's all it was to me. The money wasn't great. It wasn't even good. But it was OK. And that was OK with me.

It was a job. A job comes along, you take it. I took it.

They approached me. I didn't approach them. They came to me. One at a time. Both of them. I don't know how they found me, but they found me.

I asked them how they found me. It's the kind of thing you like to know. You like to know how people find you. So I asked them. I asked him first because he found me first, or at least I assumed he found me first. I asked him how he found me. He gave me some story or other that made little or no sense to me, so I told him, that story makes little or no sense to me. So he told me another story. It was the same story. It was starting to make sense.

I asked her too. I told her I wanted to know how she found me. She told me the same thing he had told me twice, only out of her mouth it sounded different. I didn't know who to believe.

So I believed them both. I believed them both and I didn't believe either of them. I believed him, but not her. I believed her, but not him. I believed what I wanted to believe.

He approached me first and I didn't ask him what he wanted, he told me. He said nothing, and that said plenty. I guessed what he had on his mind. Call it ESP, call it telepathy, call it what you will, I knew. How did I know? He told me. He told me nothing.

She said a little more, and that wasn't much. She said that she had come to see me about the same thing that he had seen me about. I told her to go on. So she told me a little more. A little more than nothing. Very little more.

When I pieced together the little that she had told me and everything he didn't tell me, it started to add up to something. I wasn't sure what, though. You're never sure that early on.

Look, it was a job. And in my position I was in no position to turn down a job. What position was that? I needed a job.

It's rather unorthodox to accept the same job twice, from two different parties, but neither of them seemed to mind. In fact, it was the only way they'd have it. So I accepted the same job twice and we were all happy.

Basically, it was this. He wanted me to watch her. He also wanted me to watch him and her together. She wanted me to watch him, and she also wanted me to watch her and him together. I was supposed to watch. Just watch. Don't ask any questions, don't bother with conclusions, just watch.

They didn't actually say it in those words, but that's how I read it. I considered the proposition and said, if it's me you want, I'm your man. We shook hands. I shook hands with her. I shook hands with him. They shook hands with each other.

So that's how it started. Or at least that's how I think it started. But it always starts some time before you think it's starting. Way before.

There's no middle here. Just a beginning and an end. There's no middle because it was an open and shut case.

I kept my part of the bargain. Did what I was told to do. Kept my eyes on them and didn't ask any questions. Kept my eyes on them and didn't make any judgments, didn't come to any conclusions. That's what I did and that's all I did.

The job was a piece of cake. No complications. I did what I was told to do until they told me to stop.

They thanked me and we settled up. They paid me what we had agreed upon, plus expenses. I took it.

I took it, and I took something else too. I took it because I wanted it. I took it because I needed it. And I took it because I figured I had it coming to me.

I took a short nap.

For a Glimpse of Eternity

I've learned that I'm wanted—dead or alive. How did this turn of events come about? Did I commit an offense, or am I just being defensive? Was I in the right place at the wrong time, with one finger in the orifice of eternity, or had I merely put a finger to the pulse of time, hoping to fill the void (it's my void and I'll do what I want) with problems, or perhaps a meaningless death?

Might I be mistaken? Did I actually give the finger to eternity, flip the bird to the ages, as it were, or was it just my imagination? What's the problem? What's my problem? What's yours? A perfect Manhattan, neat? Will you settle for an imperfect Brooklyn, messy?

I've got a great big paradigm shift in the works, toiling away at eternity after years of slaving away at the small details, the minor ones, the insignificant ones. Ah, eternity—that was my first mistake, my Achilles heel! I should have stuck to what I knew, or, at least, could imagine. Write about what you know, they told me, that's the first rule. The cardinal rule. The oriole rule. But another voice told me to up the ante, to sign the contract with the infinite, and there I rose to the challenge, hoisted my quill, and stepped out of my league.

Or did I? I think I know just about as much of eternity as anybody in this hick burg known as the here and now. I had been suckered by the promise of—not vast riches, no, something more seductive, the chance for a glimpse of an abstract perfection. Just a glimpse. I acknowledged the futility, but refused give up hope.

So here I am, with a price on my head, a significant markdown, no less, and nowhere to run to, baby, nowhere to hide. Waiting for what may or may not be the inevitable, my appointment with Destiny.

Then, as soon as I said it, she walked through the door: Destiny Lamour, *my* Destiny.

"You're fifteen minutes late," I told her.

"What's fifteen minutes compared to eternity?" she replied. Then she raised her pistol and plugged me so full of holes that I can't

About the Author

Called "one of the innovators of the short short story" by *Publishers Weekly*, Peter Cherches is a writer, singer and lyricist. Over the past 40 years his writing, both fiction and nonfiction, has appeared in dozens of magazines, anthologies and websites. His first recording as a jazz vocalist, *Mercerized! Songs of Johnny Mercer*, was released in 2016. He is the author of three previous prose collections, including *Lift Your Right Arm* and *Autobiography Without Words,* both published by Pelekinesis. Cherches is a native of Brooklyn, New York.

112 Harvard Ave #65
Claremont, CA 91711 USA

pelekinesis@gmail.com
www.pelekinesis.com
Pelekinesis titles are available through Small
Press Distribution, Baker & Taylor, Ingram,
Bertrams, and directly from the publisher's
website.